Spartacus
The Gods Demand Sacrifice

Robert Southworth

Published in 2013 by FeedARead.com Publishing –
Arts Council funded

A CIP catalogue record for this title is available from
the British Library.

'Thank you Pixie'

Prologue

69 B.C was coming to an end and though Rome was devoid of a figurehead, they still expanded, hungrily devouring lands. With each passing sunrise, it engorged itself upon the territories and people of those within easy striking distance. State, nation and empire all looked on, fearful of which of them, the horde from Rome would turn its attention towards next. The tribes of Gaul who had already suffered the loss of land to the legions, seemed the obvious choice. However, many leaders of once powerful kingdoms could feel the cold ice-like shiver down their spine, knowing that if Rome did indeed decide to take their lands, then there would be little to stop them. Ptolemy was one such ruler; he watched mournfully the sunrise from his royal barge. He wished these could be more settled times, especially as he glanced down at his sleeping child. The new-born child Cleopatra knew nothing of the troubles which faced her father's kingdom. Egypt was once a mighty nation, able to draw upon a fine army and enormous wealth, but those days were passed. His spies had told of how Rome operated, there was no King, Pharaoh or Emperor, and yet it still functioned. Even more surprising was that his men informed

him that the Senate as it was called was full to the very brim of corrupt men intent on power at any costs, they robbed, cheated and murdered and yet Rome flourished. Most of those men observed caused a response of nothing more than scorn from his spies. However, the names of two men kept arising. Marcus Lucinius Crassus of whom Ptolemy had actually had dealings, the man was shrewd, deceitful and extremely intelligent. At the time, Ptolemy had met him the Egyptian leader had made a mental note to be careful of the man, but now it seems the Roman senator gained far more power and influence. He had developed into an extremely dangerous man, one which Ptolemy knew would look to his lands. They were rich in grain, a necessity for any ambitious empire. The other man was Gnaeus Pompeius Magnus a completely different character to Crassus but just as deadly. An expert on the battlefield, he too had seen his wealth; power and influence expand to the point where he may take the step to seize complete control of Rome. One day Ptolemy knew that these men or men like them would come, and has he stroked his sleeping child's face, he wondered what the future held for her. He glanced out once more to the banks of the Nile, sighing he muttered to himself,

'They will come, but not for many years. They will look north and so we have time.'

Another figure which thought merely of buying more time approached the villa of Pompey. Cassian had left his household after just a few days, so he could deliver his report to his master in person. Pompey observed Cassian arrive and uncharacteristically rushed out to meet his young employee, for his own spies had already informed him of the great feats that Cassian, and his men had succeeded in achieving. Pompey clasped Cassian; this was indeed a shock. Pompey was not a socially outgoing man, much preferring the life of a soldier, to that of the Senate. He stepped away still smiling at the serious young man before him.

'Your journey back to these shores went well, I trust.' asked Pompey.

'Yes, my lord.'

'And your injury, it mends well?'

'As the weather becomes colder, it becomes a nuisance,' replied Cassian his hand involuntarily dropping to his thigh.

'Part of soldiering, my shoulder still grumbles like an old dog when the frost lies upon the ground.'

Cassian never replied but merely smiled, it was invariably awkward talking with a man who could wipe him from the world, and he had constantly adopted the strategy to say, as little as possible.

'So Cassian, how shall we make use of you and your men?'

'I would like some time to be with my family and men. I owe both parties much.'

'Your losses were substantial I understand?'

'Many good men gave their lives to see this task completed.'

'What of the gladiator Spartacus?' Pompey questioned his tone becoming distinctly more serious.

Cassian had feared this moment, he knew that Pompey may well simply order the former leader of the slave rebellion put to death now that Dido was rotting in the earth.

'Spartacus is a man of great skills and honour, without him the mission would have failed. I would never have returned like so many of my unfortunate men.'

'You trust this man?'

'More than any other,' replied Cassian. Within that simple statement, Cassian had bound his fate to that of Spartacus, he had declared that his loyalty belonged to the gladiator.

'It would be interesting to meet this man.'

'I feel that may give rise to certain issues, after all you did order his child slain.'

Pompey smiled, clearly this Spartacus wished him dead,

'The needs of Rome can be cruel Cassian,' he paused, 'very well keep this gladiator close or send him far away, either way you are responsible for his actions.'

Cassian nodded his agreement; Pompey had made it obvious that if Spartacus was to misbehave, then Cassian would be the one to accept the blame. For a moment neither spoke, Pompey lost in concentration for a moment, his mind returning to the issue of Crassus.

'You realise that Crassus is an extremely vindictive man?' The leader of so many men suddenly showed concern upon his face, for just one of his foot soldiers.

'I do, I was hoping your protection would be enough to dissuade him from retribution.'

'I will of course do all I can, but you have to see that Crassus' loathing for me will make him try all the harder to make an example of you. He will be determined to take revenge for the slight you have inflicted upon him.'

'Then I must take care and prepare.'

'You will have time, he will not rush. He is like the cat who likes to play with his prey.'

'Then he should take care, this prey might bite back.'

'Good man,' laughed Pompey, though in truth, he was taken aback by the change in the young man before him. 'I consider you a valuable member of my staff Cassian. I would have that arrangement continue.'

'Thank you, general.'

With that the meeting was ended, almost in a dream-like state Cassian found himself riding away from the Pompey's villa. The conversation had been filled with many words, but they had confirmed what Cassian believed to be the case long before he met the great general. The fact was, Cassian and his men were alone and Crassus will send his killers, eager to remove the man who wronged him. Already Cassian was planning his future actions, his spies would seek more information while he spent valuable time with his family. As he rode the first cold white flakes of snow nestled upon the ground.

Chapter I

The world was at peace. With the intense snows' anger and plans for war were driven away. The lands slept for the unusually heavy fall of snow had taken all by surprise, and they struggled to break free from its cold embrace. The birds were silent and flightless, not venturing into the cold. Animals sheltered where they could, gathered close to one another to guard against the bitter chill which accompanied the serene winter flakes. Inside the white covered buildings, people copied the beasts, huddled next to one another around large open fires. They consumed ample quantities of wine to warm from within. Only slave footprints could be seen in the snow. Wood was required for the fires and provisions needed for the banqueting table, their masters still needed nourishment.

In one such household, the slaves were happier, or it would be better to say, more comfortable. It would be a clear over statement to suggest a slave could ever truly be happy, only freedom could bring about that state. However, their master returned from his task the previous year a changed man. The squalid quarters they had once frequented had been demolished with an entirely new building being erected. The structure guarded well against the cold and yet remained light and welcoming to those who dwelt within. New clothes, including cloaks, were provided. They had no idea why their master had become so generous, but thanked the reason behind it, for a slave must take any small luxury that came their way.

Cassian slept an uneasy slumber. The nightmares of a powerful man demanding revenge haunted him regularly now. Only the special herbs' Aegis prepared for him took the edge from the blades which pierced his times of rest. He had hoped his patron would protect him but, upon meeting with the man; it was made clear that he must look to his own defence. He woke once again, with beads of sweat tracing down his face. Cassian glanced to the door which led to the adjoining room where his wife, now expecting their third child, slept. He thanked the Gods; she did not witness his nights of turmoil. He would not allow his troubles to burden her, especially whilst she was carrying their child. Cassian spoke to Aegis of his dreams believing the man to possess a gift for soothing the spirit. The gentle giant had done what he could, praying to the Gods and mixing a special brew, but still the nightmares continued. Aegis had gone to the other men and told

11

them of Cassian's visions. To a man, they chose to stay longer. If Cassian's visions were indeed a premonition of things to come, then they would all stay at their friend's side. When Cassian enquired as to why they remained they blamed the weather. It was a convenient excuse; the winter provided a heavy white blanket which lay across the land, causing many within the Empire to postpone travel. If Cassian guessed they were not being entirely honest with him, he never let his suspicions be known. If the truth be told, Cassian was happy they would remain, for the future worried him. He was not concerned for himself, he had grown accustomed to danger, but his thoughts were for his family.

Spartacus kissed his sleeping daughter revelling in the time he could spend with his family. His wife, Cynna, lay on the bed next to him, her long red hair flowing onto her naked shoulders. He ran his fingers down the smooth skin of her back, marvelling at her beauty. Her slight, involuntary movement showed her delight at his touch. She turned her head, and her smile was broad and welcoming. She gently kissed his powerful hand, and then her gaze became more serious,

You must speak with Cassian. Epionne becomes concerned for him.'

'Women are always looking to know a man's mind,' Spartacus jested, 'besides she's his wife, why doesn't she talk to him?'

'And you're his friend, and some thing's men like to keep from their wives, as you are well aware.' Her tone was earnest and Spartacus knew this would be a battle he could not win. He held up his hands in false surrender,

'You are the victor, I will speak with him later.'

'He will be taking his stroll around the grounds now,' she pressed.

Spartacus emitted a sigh, he leapt from the bed after first catching his wife with a well aimed slap on the buttocks. She let out a playful squeal, and with a tell-tale grin that made him aware that she would eagerly wait for his to return.

Spartacus picked his way through the snow; he knew where Cassian would be. As tricky and hard as he was to pin down in his business dealings, Cassian was always predictable in his home life. True to form he could be found leaning against a tree surveying his property. Spartacus trudged the small incline to where his friend stood in deep contemplation, Cassian completely unaware of his approach.

'Tell me, what is it?' Spartacus asked, his face wearing a look which announced he would not be persuaded from his question.

'It's the silence,' replied Cassian, not turning to face Spartacus but still gazing out across his lands.

'I have told you before Cassian, I'm a fighter, do not speak in riddles.'

'I have men out there, trying to find out what Crassus is up to, but nothing not even whispers on the wind,' replied Cassian, this time turning to look at Spartacus.

'But surely that's a good thing?' Spartacus replied, confused by Cassian's concerns.

'There are always whispers Spartacus, even if only faint. Unless,' Cassian suddenly paused, mid sentence, as though to utter the remaining words would make his terrible dreams become a reality.

'There's a man in the employ of Crassus, who is so feared above all, not even my agents would risk angering him. For his methods are vile and cruel, and the man has never failed.'

'Then we just kill the man,' Spartacus replied. His bravado always came to the front when danger reared from the darkness. Cassian just shrugged,

'You don't kill Titus Flabinus. He kills you, your family, your friends, even you bloody dog. The man is not of this world, he is unstoppable.'

Spartacus stared at Cassian. He had never seen his friend like this, so defeated and seemingly without a plan, he always had a plan.

'Listen, if this man has been set upon us, then we need to know, and we need to find a way of besting him.' The words brought no response from Cassian but his silence brought a burning anger to Spartacus. 'Cassian if you want to sit around and be slaughtered like swine that's up to you. However, your family and mine deserve a chance, an opportunity to be free of this man's attention,' Spartacus paused to add weight to his words, 'I suggest we call the men together and speak with them. They must know of the dangers we all face.'

'Of course forgive me!' Cassian's mind suddenly snapped back into reality. He realised all the camp must prepare if the worst of his nightmares were to come true. After all, it was not just his family who faced this threat, but all who were called a friend by his household.

He asked Spartacus to walk with him, and as they ambled around the snow-covered fields, he went through all that he knew of Flabinus. He talked of the rumours and of whole families, which had been removed from the face of the world by the man. He recounted the tale of Demotrates, a rising star in the world of trading who succeeded in agreeing bargaining terms with the Gaul tribes, who had for so long resisted trade with Rome. Many failed but not Demotrates, he did not know the meaning of the word.

'He was brilliant, such intelligence. His love for making a deal was only eclipsed by his love for his family. I knew him for just a short time, but I learnt more in his presence at about trading than I had ever learnt before or since.'

'What happened?' Spartacus replied, almost fearing the answer.

'One of his trading deals went against Crassus' wishes. Then, one day, the man returned to his home after a prosperous endeavour to find his family butchered.'

'Is that so unusual in these times?' Spartacus had heard stories like this before.

'You don't understand, not just his wife and child but his entire family. The slaves, who attended his household, even the animals that grazed upon his land were all torn apart. When he returned to his warehouses to gather men for retribution, all his men had been dispatched to the next world. It must have been as if his entire life had been erased before his very eyes.'

'By the Gods!' Spartacus was aghast at the words Cassian spoke.

'In a just a few hours Demotrates lost his family, his home and his life's work.'

'And the man himself?'

'He would not give Crassus the lasting victory, before the men of Flabinus could get to him, he lay in the ruins of his home, his beloved at his side and opened a vein. He would meet his family on his own terms and not at the order of Crassus.'

'A small victory but a victory none the less, personally I would have opened the guts of this man Crassus,' Spartacus replied thoughtfully.

'No matter how skilled with a blade, nobody gets close to Crassus.'

As the two walked the perimeter, they became aware they were not alone, a figure held the shadows and the cover afforded to him by the trees. Spartacus cursed himself for not wearing his sword, a luxury he had felt comfortable in doing these last few months. He would not make that mistake again, from this day forwards his blade would never leave his side.

'We should retire behind the walls of the villa, we do not know if he is alone.' But, as Spartacus spoke, Cassian was already striding purposely towards the uninvited guest.

'Stay your aggression Cassian, for I mean no malice.' The figure spoke when Cassian was but a few feet away.

'Druro!' Cassian exclaimed. 'What would the eyes of Crassus be doing on my lands?'

'I bring warning. The wolf has been unleashed, come the melting of the snows he will come.'

'Why would you give this information freely?' Cassian replied, whilst observing the man, searching for some act of trickery.

'Let me say the information I gather has caused too many innocents to die, I care not for the methods of Flabinus. It was on my information that Demotrates and many like him have suffered.

I have been asked to gather such information on you Cassian, and you have little time before I must hand over all that I have learnt.'

'And who does this information concern?'

'You must safeguard the household of Crannicus too, but you have so little time. Cassian you should run, run fast and keep running. Do not stop, for the wolf will not until he has caught and devoured you.' The figure turned and trudged through the snows to a waiting horse, he nodded and was gone. Spartacus watched the figure leave,

'Do you think we can trust him?' he asked.

'What choice do we have? I can't see that his warning to us could benefit his master in any way, it just gives us more time to prepare,' replied Cassian.

The fire roared as all were seated around the substantial table. At the tables head sat Cassian and he waited for the talk to stop. As usual Epionne was the last to notice that she was holding up proceedings. She glanced at her husband expecting a look or word to reprimand her, but he just smiled lingering a while upon her gaze. Cassian began slowly, talking of the events of the previous mission and how that mission had brought his family to the notice of Crassus.

'I had hoped that the protection of our patron Pompey would dissuade Crassus from retribution, but I fear I was mistaken.' Cassian clasped his hands to his head fearing to tell those he loved the terrible position he had placed them in. Epionne rose and moved quickly to his side to comfort him.

'What is it my love?'

Spartacus now began to speak,

'Crassus has given orders that Cassian be made an example of. His family, friends and home will all be forfeit. He plans to remove this household from the world, he would wipe its name from history if he could.'

'Not while I still stand,' Bull raised himself from the table, 'you have my sword Cassian!'

The statement and sentiment was echoed by each and everyone at the table. Cassian looked at his friends who so readily faced death and was humbled by the display. Spartacus then quietened the mood, dragging his friends back from joyous deviance.

'It is settled then, we will stand side by side. Cassian we will need information on this wolf Crassus has set upon us. Also will we stay here or attempt to leave these lands?'

Epionne suddenly gasped,

20

'Cassian what about Flora?'

'They travel here as I speak. Even before I had confirmation who had been sent against us, I had made it clear to Crannicus that he should join us. Despite his complaints he finally relented, and will be here by the morning, unless Druro's words were false and Flabinus has struck already.'

Far to the south the city of Utica was transformed; legal traders came from all over the known world to carve out new business interests. As the city grew from strength to strength so did a certain young warrior. Plinius had finished his morning exercise, he no longer felt tired to the point of collapse after only a mild exertion. Each day he became stronger and also more frustrated at being caged up. Plinius would forever be in Stoiclese's debt, but the young man needed to be upon his way. He had need to see his friends and, even more importantly, Chia. He imagined their faces when his friends set eyes upon him and he smiled. Chia's face visited him constantly and he hoped she had not found another, for that wound would be more difficult to heal than any caused by a swords thrust. The sudden thought of it made him seek out Stoiclese, for the time had come to say goodbye to the old healer and to Utica. He entered a small room. Charts and documents

21

covered every available space and there, studying one such document, was Stoiclese. The man never seemed to sleep. Before Plinius could speak the hunched figure stood and smiled,

'So the time has come young Plinius?'

'I can never thank you enough, only I would ask one more favour,' the young man looked sheepish as he spoke.

'Your friend Aegis has supplied funds for your travel, and much more to aid you on your journey,' replied Stoiclese guessing at Plinius' concerns.

The relief, which was clearly showing on the young man's face, made Stoiclese's smile broaden,

'You don't think I would nurse you back to health, only to see you starve upon the way home?' They clasped arms and said their farewells, Stoiclese had grown to like the young warrior but wondered how long the man before him would stay safe. He had talent with a blade and a growing reputation, a mixture which was likely to lead to trouble.

The sun shone brightly, Utica was not experiencing the cold of the Roman lands to the north, in fact Plinius had decided against wearing his armour, a simple tunic would suffice. His armours weight still tired him too quickly, so he paid to have his belongings carried to the docks where he would board a vessel to Caralis. He couldn't help smiling to himself, soon he would meet those he yearned to see and marry Chia if she would still have him. Nerves gripped him, if only he had recovered quicker.

The days had passed too quickly for Cassian. He glanced into the courtyard, the sun was beginning to melt the snow; he prayed that the cold would last just a little while longer. He needed time to formulate his plans, he tried to remain positive but this man Flabinus was no ordinary foe. He would not listen to reason he thought only of blood. Cassian knew if he did not prepare well enough then all would be lost. A shout split the air and Cassian rushed to the gates. There, in the distance, a convoy moved slowly towards his home. Spartacus joined him and together they rode out to meet the convoy, joy in their hearts that the household of Crannicus had negotiated their way safely. Tictus headed the convoy and, with Flora, he rode to greet Cassian and Spartacus.

'My dear Cassian. Only the Gods know how pleased I am to see you,' Flora said quietly, the relief evident upon her face.

'Where is Crannicus?' Cassian asked, immediately fearing the answer.

'He would not leave, he said he would not allow these men to destroy my gardens.'

'Is he mad?' Cassian cried exasperated, 'What are gardens compared to the safety of his life?'

This time Tictus spoke,

'I pleaded with my father, but he would have none of it.'

'Oh Cassian! What am I to do without my husband?'

'I will fetch him,'

Cassian turned and made to ride away. But Spartacus grasped at Cassian's mount and refused to release his hold, despite Cassian's attempts to break free.

'You are needed here. Make your plans I will be back in five days.' Cassian saw the determination in his friend's eyes and knew there would be no argument and besides Spartacus spoke the truth, he required all the time possible to prepare for what they must do.

'Very well but be quick, the snows begin to melt.' Cassian's words were harsher than he meant and he quickly added 'Be careful Spartacus, this man is one of the most dangerous in Rome.' Spartacus nodded then grabbed some supplies from the convoy, and galloped to the horizon cursing the stupidity of Crannicus. Deep down he admired the man's love for his wife. He would risk all for a smile from his beloved, despite the fellow's vulgarity he had shown himself to be generous in both love and spirit. Now he must convince the man to forget his honour and run, for only in running did any of them have a hope of survival.

Chapter II

Plinius entered the former headquarters of the tyrant Apelios. The guard had seemed a little thrown when Plinius had approached him. Plinius remembered the man from his training at the home of Albus, and the man obviously recognised Plinius now standing at his front. He simply shrank away, not wanting conversation and so Plinius, a smile upon his face, had been able to enter the building without uttering a single word. As he walked along the marbled corridor, a man emerged from a room to his right. Plinius enquired to the whereabouts of Albus. The man, obviously in a rush, just gestured over his shoulder and hurriedly disappeared through one of the many doors. Plinius knocked but no reply came, so he gently slipped inside to observe a man deep in concentration, his mind firmly locked on the many documents upon his desk. Plinius gave a subtle cough, trying to catch the man's attention. Without looking up Albus muttered some curse, pointed out he did not want to be disturbed and waved a hand to dismiss whoever had entered, still without raising his head.

'Forgive me Albus, I had hoped you could tell me whereabouts of my friends.'

Albus looked up, his face instantly losing its previous colour. He struggled to stand, not knowing whether to run or to throw an object at the spectre which presented itself in front of him. Plinius held up his hand trying to calm the old soldier,

'Albus I am as real as you. I have spent many days since the tournament recovering from my injuries.'

'But Cassian...he said you were slain in the arena,' Albus managed to stutter, his face the colour of highly polished white marble, unsure whether to trust his senses. Maybe all these endless documents had finally taken their toll and made him lose his mind.

'He believed me to be so. Aegis pulled me from the corpse pile when few would have spotted life in me. Stoiclese has worked his magic, and so I stand before you.' He smiled at Albus trying to reassure him. Spying some wine on the desk, he quickly filled a goblet and handed it to the man. Albus reluctantly took it, drinking the contents down in one and then refilling it immediately,

'It is really you?'

'I am truly here Albus, and I only seek to be reunited with my friends and Chia.' Plinius smiled as finally, the old soldier began to

27

relax. Albus and Plinius talked for some time, discussing what had taken place after the victory in the tournament. They talked of Chia and how she left with Cassian after being freed, wanting to honour Plinius' name. When at last they parted, Plinius made straight for the docks to obtain passage, which would see him finally be reunited with the woman he loved.

Far away in the city of Rome, Druro sat playing with his young son. The boy was progressing well with his education and deserved some quality time with his father. His servant rushed into the room,

'Forgive me! However, Marcus Licinius Crassus is here.' Even a slave knew the importance of the man. Druro leapt to his feet sending the boy's toys sprawling across the highly polished floor.

'Take the boy to his mother and send wine.' The servant moved quickly to remove the young child, but before he completed the task, Druro cried 'Wait!' and bent down on one knee. He kissed his son and held him for a moment,

'Go quickly!'

He turned and let the child go with the servant, feeling a chill enter his bones as he knew danger had entered his home. Crassus entered the modest house of Druro and glanced around at his surroundings. He thought the gutter rat had done well from being in his employ. Druro rushed from one of the adjoining rooms,

'Crassus! Forgive me, I was unaware we had a meeting today.'

'Oh all men must pay a visit to their loyal supporters.' The emphasis on word 'loyal' hit its target hard and; in that moment, Druro knew all was lost. He straightened his back, for the first time he would not allow this man to force him to hide in the shadows and tremble at his every word.

'You spoke with Cassian?' Crassus eyed the man before him, his guilt was not in question, however, as yet; he had not decided his fate.

'Yes.' There was no apology in Druro's response, merely defiance.

'And why would you do this?' Crassus asked, eyeing the man keenly though in truth, no answer would save the man who stood before him.

'Killing a man in this business is part of the game we all play. However, what happened to Demotrates was not. I would at least give Cassian the chance to prepare for his fate. Wiping a man and his family from history shames us Crassus.' replied Druro, his words masking the very real terror he felt inside.

'You show yourself to be a man of honour, a rare quality in these times. I commend you Druro and as such, by way of reward; you have two days.'

'Two days, my lord?' Druro asked, his heart in his mouth as he spoke.

'Two days, before you are added to the list of Flabinus. It seems he will be busy in the coming weeks, though i doubt he will complain.'

Crassus spoke no more, he turned and strode from the household of Druro. The deal was done, the death sentence passed without pomp or ceremony.

Druro slumped to his knees, fearing but knowing what the future held in store for his family. The door creaked behind making him jump with fear. The cheeky face of his son smiled back at him, the boy's obvious delight at giving the slave the slip was evident. Druro beckoned his son to him with a smile, hugging him; he whispered into his ear,

'Let's go on an adventure.' The boy whooped with joy, unaware of the tears which travelled snake-like down his father's cheek.

Spartacus cursed his luck, having to ride all the way back to Cassian's villa, with this bloated ox continuously complaining. It had taken longer than he had intended to lever Crannicus from his home and only when forced to draw his sword and use threats did the fool agree to vacate his villa. Even then he continued to bellow insult after insult, and it was beginning to grate on Spartacus' nerves.

'Cassian will hear of your threats.' Crannicus complained.

'What is that to me?' Spartacus was only partly listening to the ramblings of the man, he knew they travelled a dangerous road and so kept his mind and his eyes on spotting any danger, which threatened them.

'You serve him, and if I was your master.' The words were meant to sting for Crannicus knew full well, Spartacus was no slave.

'Maybe I should simply gut you now. I could easily tell the others I was just too late.' Spartacus stared at Crannicus and watched the man wilt physically and change his mind about speaking. The man simply looked back towards his home; this did not go unnoticed by Spartacus, who felt a stab of pity for the man.

31

'Understand Crannicus, the assassin who comes for us, is no ordinary foe.'

'But my home, Flora did so love it.' Crannicus seemed resigned to its destruction.

'It was a beautiful home, but a home is made of stone, people are not. Your wife and son would rather have you by their side.' As time passed, the ground began to rise, and they were treated to the spectacle of the surrounding countryside. Both the homes of Crannicus to the rear and the household of Cassian to the front were out of sight, but the length of view made them both feel like they sat just around the corner. It was Spartacus who spotted the smoke first; it began as slight wisps but then the dark foreboding clouds rose, in earnest, and as Crannicus watched, he knew his home was no more. Anger flared within him but he was powerless, and secretly he was thankful he was not present when the blaze started.

As Spartacus and Crannicus watched, another set of eyes saw the fate of the home of Crannicus, and his heart was filled with terror. Plinius had covered the ground quickly as he urgently sought reunion with Chia. It came as a shock as he neared the villa of Crannicus to see the flames rising from it, and figures dressed all in black looting its possessions. Only four of them had remained inside, while another four had set off north. The reason for which Plinius did not know, but was determined to discover. Plinius changed into his armour; he had no way of knowing whether Chia or his friends were inside and what had become of them. He picked his way down to the villa, ensuring firstly no other enemy were close by, he didn't draw his swords but held on tightly to a javelin. Screams of delight came from those inside. As he rounded the main doorway he observed one of the men stamping on the flower beds in just a mindless act of destruction. There were no bodies and Plinius guessed Crannicus and his household had left, somehow knowing that trouble was upon them. Plinius was about to leave as the flower destroying rider smashed the head from one of the beautiful statues. This act filled Plinius with an almost uncontrollable surging rage. He could have just walked away but he hated these men and what they had done to such a beautiful home, his mind was set.

The javelin released from Plinius' hand and soared through the air. It reached the pinnacle of its height and began to drop, accelerating as it hurtled forward. The point took the man through the centre of his back, and as he screamed his pain, the javelin pinned him to the statue that he had so delighted in partly destroying. His three comrades turned as one, rounding on Plinius, eager for retribution,

'Who the fuck are you?' one of them said, spittle releasing from his mouth as he did so. 'You will regret your actions.'

'This household is the property of my friends, you are unwelcome,' replied Plinius, his voice calm and his stare unwavering. The three drew their weapons almost simultaneously and the ground between themselves and Plinius began to shrink.

'You don't know who you are dealing with boy. Frightened are you child?'

'You are dead men, and I don't fear the dead.' Plinius drew his weapons and charged. Though they had the numerical advantage Plinius was fighting men more used to slitting throats than undertaking proper battle. They fell with ease, not able to match the skill or power of their opponent, their confidence evaporating as their blood splashed upon the ground. The warrior glanced about and saw the fire taking hold. For all his valiant efforts the villa would be lost, its beauty gone forever from this world. He mounted his horse, gathering a spare mount from those he had slain. He would need to ride hard, he would need to inform Cassian of what has happened here today.

Crannicus had not spoken since he had observed the smoke rising far behind him, he looked confused as to why all this was happening. Spartacus knew better than interrupt his thoughts. Besides Spartacus had his eyes to the front; he had seen a family making their way in the direction of Cassian's villa, and wondered who they might be. More worryingly he noticed riders trailing their progress, the family were unaware of the threat and gradually Spartacus saw the riders were beginning to close in from both sides. Spartacus wondered if it was prudent to get involved, he did not know the people in the valley. But even as he declared the fact to himself that it made sense to stay out of sight, he had encouraged his horse forward,

'Crannicus you must wait undercover, if I don't return then you must make your way to Cassian's villa but be warned there are dangers on the road.' With that Spartacus urged his horse on even harder, there would no time to be careful, he needed to close the distance quickly. The family had just become aware of the danger but could do nothing as the riders dismounted and formed a ring of blades around them. Slowly the ring closed, three men and a

35

female drew weapons and kept the child behind them. Spartacus let out a terrible roar as he arrived, scattering some of the enemy but the others pressed on with their objective. The battle was a blur to Spartacus. He knew he took at least four of the enemy down and when quiet settled, to replace the screams that had just rung out, the ground was soaked with blood and littered with bodies. Spartacus recognised Druro, he was still standing but held a hand tight to a deep slash to his thigh. The three that had stood with him lay dead about him, the child crying at the woman's body. Druro crossed to his son,

'Come we must leave.'

The child screamed out its confusion, not wanting to the body of the fallen woman.

Druro's actions seemed stern in the way he pulled the boy from what Spartacus guessed was its mother. However, the way in which Druro then held him close and tried to comfort the child, was evidence to Spartacus that man loved the boy and would grieve the woman at a less perilous time. But not now, not while his son was still in mortal danger. Crannicus joined them shortly, though upon finding out who Druro's former employer was, refused point blank to converse with the man. Rounding up the horses took time but eventually they set off. The bodies of Druro's wife and slaves were tied to the backs of their horses, the lifeless forms of the black riders remained where they died in the dirt. Riders and mounts moved away quickly, not knowing how many further enemy still lurked dangerously close. They were all anxious, continuously scanning the horizon for tell tale signs of imminent attack. Eventually though they reached the relative safety of Cassian's villa without any further incident, and the relief on all their faces was clear to see.

Later that day the sun was setting as the four dark clad riders who had previously been at the villa of Crannicus stopped their horses, a good distance away from the villa. It was a good vantage point and they could clearly observe Cassian's property. They had seen the carnage where some of their comrades had fallen, but it was impossible to tell what damage they had done in return.

'Should we go and report to Flabinus?' One of them asked, fearing that he too would experience the fate shared by his fallen comrades.

'No! His orders were simple enough, we were just supposed to observe. See what the bastards were up to.'

'But-'

'Look we move from this spot and Flabinus will cut our balls off. In a few days he will be here with all the men. Then there will be a reckoning down there with the bastards who killed our men,' he spat on the floor as he finished speaking.

The watchers were unaware that they too were being observed. Plinius had caught up with them and followed them to their vantage point. Now he lay concealed, close enough to hear every word they uttered.

Plinius had heard all he needed to know. The plan of the men before him was to sit and wait for a larger force, then an attack on the villa would follow. He slowly slipped his weapons from their scabbards, he had no intention of allowing them to fulfil their plans. The man who spat watched the arch of his spit as it landed just in front of a bush. His eyes did a double take as the bush seemed to come alive as if being angered by his action. The glint of a blade was a warning received too late as it cut across his face, taking both eyes from him. He screamed his agony and rolled away from his attacker, calling for his comrades to help him. Help could not come for each of his men fell to the blade of Plinius, their screams startling the birds from the trees. Spartacus and Cassian stood at the walls of the villa and heard the death cries of men.

'Where the hell did those screams come from?' Bull asked as he joined them.

Both men shook their head and merely pointed in the general direction. Another scream broke the silence, and all on the wall knew somewhere in the distance men were dying. The injured man scrambled away from the approaching footsteps, the pain he felt only eclipsed by the panic stirring inside. Plinius grabbed him,

'Why are you here?' he asked, while making sure the man felt the tip of his blade.

'Just watching that's all.' The man cowered from the brute that held him, trying to pull away but the powerful grip held him firm.

'Tell me everything or you will die slow.' Plinius was almost shocked by his own actions, but he knew he must find out every possible detail from this man.

'Flabinus ordered us to destroy the home of Crannicus, and then watch the household of Cassian. He comes with a force to wipe it from the face of the world with his very hands.'

'And their families?'

'Everyone dies, the orders are both houses are to be brushed away.' The man did not want to speak the truth but knew he must and hoped, if he did so, his assailant would show him some mercy.

39

Plinius looked down at the man as his final scream again filled the air, he cleaned his blades and mounted his horse.

The men on the walls still watched for an attack, darkness was beginning to own the day and torches were lit. The screams had put an edge to the nerves, but the deathly silence which came afterwards only served to intensify the feelings of dread. Then, suddenly, a distant sound made them lean forward trying to discern its nature.

'Sounds like a horse,' Cassian whispered.

The sound became louder, clearly the cause of the noise was coming in closer. A blurred figured stopped at the very edge of the torch light, and held up his hand to show they were empty.

'Stay where you are, what is your business here?' Spartacus roared, daring the shadow to challenge his authority.

'Well I had hoped for a kinder welcome, maybe even some wine,' came the reply from out of the darkness.

'By the Gods who are you?' Cassian shouted. But Spartacus had already made his way down to the main gate and was pulling the locking bar across. 'Spartacus what the fuck are you doing?' The figure moved forward, a smile upon his face. Both Cassian and Bull gasped, disbelief overtaking their ability to talk. Spartacus raced from the villa as he did Plinius slid from his mount, the two stopped an arm's length from one another.

'But how?' Spartacus asked, struggling to speak.

'A combination of magic from Aegis and Stoiclese. I will tell all later, but I have important news.'

'Oh bollocks!' Spartacus cried out and launched himself at Plinius and embraced the man. Plinius embraced his friend back and for a moment no words were said until an embarrassed cough interrupted the moment. It was Bull,

'Sorry should we leave you two alone? Or can we lock these gates as the countryside is swarming with people who want to cut our throats.'

'It's worse than you think, at best you have two, maybe three days.'

Cassian stepped forward,

'Come inside Plinius, we need to know all you have learned.' The heavy wooden doors slammed shut, for a short time at least keeping the danger at bay. Each man had conflicting emotions, euphoria at the return of Plinius who they had believed to be dead, and deep concern for what might come from the gathering shadows.

41

Chapter III

Plinius entered the home of Cassian and the greetings came thick and fast. Aegis stood to his front. Plinius owed his very life to him and for just one moment there was an awkward silence between them. Then the silence was broken,

'It is good to see you young Plinius.' Aegis said, a huge broad grin upon his face. He held out his hand but Plinius brushed it aside embracing the man, mere words could not express his gratitude. The room erupted into cheers. Spartacus began to question Aegis and Plinius on how this could be, but Plinius held up his hand,

'Forgive me my friends, but first I must ask; where is Chia?'

'She rarely comes from her room once the day is at an end,' Cassian replied.

Epionne stepped forward and kissed Plinius gently on the cheek,

'Go to her. She is in great need of the man she loves.'

She then took him by the hand and led him through the household. For some reason Plinius expected to go to the slave quarters, however his route took him to the very centre of the villa, an area which spoke of wealth and good taste. Epionne stopped at a door and gestured to Plinius; she winked and left without a word. Plinius gulped down his nerves, his hand raised to knock the door but he thought better of it and he slowly, almost reluctantly, slipped inside.

The room was beautiful with only a little light. His eyes adjusted to the darkness and he spied a figure lying on the bed. The figure faced away from him. He made to speak but the figure, without moving, spoke before he could utter any words,

'Forgive me Epionne, I don't feel like company tonight.' Plinius thought he heard a tremble in the girl's voice,

'That is a shame, for I have wanted your company for a long time.'

The figure stiffened on the bed but still did not turn,

'You have visited me many times Plinius and each time I grasp for you my love, you vanish into mist'

'Not this time my love. I have returned and plan never to leave your side.'

Chia turned. So long she had held her resolve, not letting her grief overtake her, but now she sobbed. The tears flowed like the waters of the Tiber, unchecked and raw. Plinius rushed to the bed, taking her in his arms in one swift movement. He wiped the tears from her eyes with gentle fingers and kissed her, the feeling of her in his arms, the sweetest reward he could ever ask for after all the time they had been apart and all the things they had been through.

The night wore on and it was some hours later that Plinius and Chia walked hand in hand to the dining hall to join the rest of the household. As they entered all stood and saluted Plinius with their goblets and then men cheered. The women burst into tears of joy which left the men perplexed to say the least, and more than a little embarrassed.

'He's here and reunited with his love, so why bloody cry?' Bull asked, dismayed at their response.

'Don't try to understand, it will test your sanity,' Cassian replied and received a playful slap from Epionne for his remarks. For a while the group revelled in their happiness forgetting the dark clouds which were gathering, threatening a storm which would wash them from this world, within a torrent of blood and tears.

The time had come, the mood slipping from joy to concern and Cassian began the proceedings,

'Forgive me my friends, but plans must be made.' His words were simple but all present knew the weight of the statement and the room fell silent. Epionne rose and beckoned the other women to follow her but Cassian reached for her hand and held her close. preventing any further movement,

'No my love, the danger threatens all seated here and so all must play their part in the plans.' Epionne took her seat again her eyes never once straying from Cassian's.

'Firstly I must apologise for my actions have placed you all in mortal danger.'

'We have been through this Cassian, if it wasn't for you we would already be dead. We must deal with what lays ahead not in the past.' Spartacus interrupted. Cassian nodded his thanks,

'Very well. I will tell you what I know.' He paused briefly, collecting his thoughts. 'Crassus has learned of our triumph in Utica, he wishes to eradicate those who inflicted so much damage upon him. As a result he has unleashed his best man, Flabinus. This man is not the sort of wolf you want on your scent. He commands a small and very deadly army, his methods are ruthless, cruel and beyond the actions of any normal assassin. Druro have you anything to add?'

'I was responsible for gathering information upon your household and those who would help you Cassian and, unfortunately, I did it rather well. However there is a gap in that information because I insured it would be that way, and that gap, are the lands of your father. They will know from where you originate Cassian, but that is where the information ends.' Druro could not look at Cassian directly and spoke his words to the floor, his shame at the peril he had delivered to these people was a weight he could hardly bare.

'So if we were to reach my father's lands, would they stop or continue to hunt us down?'

'They will never stop Cassian, but you could buy yourself some time. Flabinus will not charge in. If you escape him he will gather information on the new target, the time it takes him to do this will perhaps give you the chance to come up with a plan, for you have none at the moment.'

'Very well. As we do not know when Flabinus will reach us-' Cassian began.

'Two days at best.' Plinius interrupted.

'How do you know this information?' Cassian asked, startled by Plinius' statement.

'I heard his scouts talking before they died, also I questioned the last one at some length. He confirmed all that I had been able to overhear a few moments before.'

'Very well, our course is set. We have no choice, we leave when the sun rises. Who will come with us? I am sure some would prefer your own path.'

The group, both man and woman declared they would stay together.

'Then I will make the arrangements. Sleep if you can, if not there will be plenty to do.'

The words Cassian spoke were the truth. The household became a swarm of activity. Decisions had to be made about personal belongings which would be taken, Epionne sometimes causing dismay at what she wished to take with her. Eventually it became too much for her and she broke down and cried. It was Flora who comforted her knowing the heartache she had suffered having to do exactly the same, just the day before. Possessions were not the only thing which posed a problem. The slaves of the housed were too numerous to take on the journey but Cassian would not leave them to the mercy of Flabinus. It was decided those that would not travel with Cassian would be sent over land, in light wagons to aid their speed, to a different port, there they would hire a ship to his father's lands. Lucius his charge hand would lead the group,

'It is important that you do not stop Lucius. You will leave shortly.' Cassian tried to impress the importance of speed upon his trusted charge hand.

'Yes my lord. What if we are captured?'

'Lucius, if this man captures you, he will kill you all. You must run. You have all the papers which will see you past any authorities. The coin I have provided you with will grant you the means to purchase passage for all. Only you have the destination on this document do not read it until you reach the port. If need be destroy it, it will be better that you hold no information which would aid our enemies.'

'Will there be anything else?' Lucius replied, wishing he was travelling with his master.

'No Lucius. Gather the people and leave now. Thank you, for all you have done.' Cassian shook the man by the hand, a gesture which was not lost on Lucius.

Cassian watched the first of the wagons pull away. He hoped they would move quickly for it was possible Flabinus would try and track down both convoys. He had sent a few armed men with them but he knew it would not make the slightest difference if they were caught. However, it may help to settle the nerves of those travelling in the wagons. He shook his head as he returned to finalize the evacuation of the rest of the household, thinking to himself of all his great schemes and how intelligent he thought he had been. More like a fool, he scolded himself privately. He faced losing everything that was dear, he should have listened to his father all those years before and stuck to the farms and trading. The thought was laughable for the empire was not a place for free choices, obedience to those with power was rarely a career path grasped by an eager student. Those with power used deceit, bribery and threats to bend the arms of those they wished to employ. Cassian's limbs were bent to breaking point before he relented and agreed to be in the service of his master. Freedom to see those you love slaughtered is a feeble freedom, and one which is seldom chosen.

They left the household with just the occasional look back, the riders that Plinius had so easily dispatched had been brought to the villa. It was a simple ruse, one which was unlikely to succeed but they would try it anyway. The bodies were placed around the villa and then a fire lit, the placement would see that enemies corpses would remain untouched by the flames, but blackened by the smoke. Luckily a few slaves within his household were not believers in funeral pyres and therefore it was possible to exhume a few bodies from the villa's cemetery, and place them in Cassian's quarters, hopefully fooling Flabinus into believing the household destroyed. The convoy moved away, lightly provisioned so there was little to slow down their progress. If the Gods smiled down on them then reaching the coast could possibly happen before Flabinus knew they were missing.

The journey was swift but hard going with the group taking few stops. The warriors were used to such feats but the pace sapped the moral of the others. Epionne still fretted over her home, sobbing often on the nearest shoulder. Cassian's son's stayed in the wagon, the confusion of the day's happenings causing considerable bewilderment and distress. Druro's son never left his father's side, preferring the uncomfortable rump of a horse to the cold frame of the wagon. The two were inseparable since the death of Druro's wife and the boy clung to his father at every possible moment. Cassian watched Druro for a while and mixed emotions raced through him. On the one hand Druro had gathered his information expertly, gathering the details for his master which would enable Flabinus to carry out his work with his usual expertise. However, on the other hand if Druro hadn't placed himself and his family in danger and warned Cassian it was likely that disaster would have befallen Cassian and his family. He doubted even the great skill of his friends could have protected his home, especially if the attack had come as night fell and the inhabitants within the villa were lazing in slumber, unaware of the peril they were in. He now had greater understanding of how Spartacus must have felt about him. After all it was Cassian who gave the order that the gladiator's son was to be slain, he must have conflicting emotions. No matter how much they had experienced together and become friends.

The scouts returned to give the news that Flabinus did not want to hear. The man was powerfully built with looks which luxurious mosaics of the Gods struggled to compete with. The Roman was handsome and strong, many men would have rested upon such gifts from the heavens but Flabinus wasn't that sort of man. He would take every opportunity to improve his intelligence, his skill with the sword and most importantly his wealth. Flabinus had plans and they would result in him never having to crawl to the likes of Crassus again. In fact maybe one day it would be Crassus on his stomach before Flabinus. The scout explained the villa had been virtually destroyed, and the remains of bodies had been discovered. Flabinus urged his horse into a gallop eager to see for himself. His men responded to his movements, they had long learned not to wait for an order. It was as though an ominous cloud had suddenly caught the wind as it hurtled towards the blackened shell that was once the household of Cassian.

Flabinus picked through the wreckage of the villa, his keen sharp eyes looking for clues as to what had occurred. He spied the corpses of his dead men and noticed no spilt blood where they lay and deep within the recesses of his mind he pieced together the truth behind the deceitful scene which had been presented to him.

'You will have to do better Cassian. This is child's play,' his words were for his own benefit.

He sent his scouts rushing to the surrounding area to look for tracks, he was sure in his own mind that Cassian and his family still lived. He was also sure that whoever had set the fire had at least two days march on them, travelling at speed and unhindered they could reach a number of ports. The scouts returned breathless and eager to share their news,

'Two sets of tracks Flabinus, setting off in different directions.'

'Very well, set camp I'm ready to eat.'

'But we may be able to catch them,' the scout spoke before thinking, it was not wise to contradict Flabinus. He quickly mumbled an apology, dreading what actions may follow.

'Not to worry,' Flabinus smiled 'I will explain my action. The ashes are cold which means those convoys, and therefore our prey, have slipped away and we will not catch them before they reach port. So we must bide our time and look for a more suitable chance for our meeting with Cassian.'

'Sorry.' The scout looked away again apologising.

'Now, bring wine!' Flabinus ordered and the scout turned immediately and ran to fetch the requested wine. Flabinus eyed the man and wondered, just for a fraction of a time, what he should do. In truth, it was a fair statement the lad had come up with. To the untrained eye it may have been worth a race to the port, but then again he led these men by fear. He really did not want them thinking for themselves. In the blink of an eye he snatched a spear from his horse and in the briefest of moments, the shaft was soaring through the air. The power of the arm which threw it was incredible, its target was unaware of the danger right up to the

53

point the spear smashed through his chest. Collapsing on the floor
the scout gasped for air as a shadow appeared above him,

'If it is alright with you, I think I will have my breakfast
now.'

Flabinus calmly walked away, discounting the fallen man's pain.
Friends of the victim, who stood helpless in the ranks, offered no
assistance. For every member of this dark army knew that if you
anger Flabinus, you do so alone.

Chapter IV

The inn was large, with ample room to take the whole of the convoy's personnel. There was no doubt it was a little run down and had seen better days, but it offered clear views of any approach that an enemy may take advantage of. It was also in close proximity to the docks so the convoy could move quickly to join Lathyrus and his vessel the very moment he arrived. Cassian paid for the rooms. Glancing around he wondered if he would be able to tell if those drinking close by could be in the employ of Flabinus. He called the owner to him,

'How much for all your rooms and no other clients?'

'What! Don't be so bloody stupid.'

'Like I said, how much?' The owner stared at him in disbelief. Clearly the man was insane or obviously had too much coin and came up with idiotic schemes to amuse himself.

'I have regulars here and some of the rooms are already occupied.' Cassian placed a large purse full of coin on the table in front of man.

'One night, the whole building. For that you get this,' Cassian gestured towards the coin purse, 'and one just like it when we leave in the morning.' Cassian eyed the man, sensing the pressure the coin had put him under; he knew the amount of coin promised would buy the tavern three times over.

'It will take me a while to empty the place.'

'Best get to it then.'

'Right you drunken bastards get out! The place is closed.' The man roared out his orders, and the grumbling from his cliental continued as they spilled out into the streets, the owner was more than happy to ignore them, the lure of the coin being too much for him.

'You know, you could have bought this place and the whole bloody street for what was in that purse.' Bull informed Cassian, shaking his head in the process.

'What good is coin to the dead? Cassian asked, 'and why on earth would I buy this place?'

'Can't argue with you there.'

Lucius was worried, it had been three days since his convoy had left his master's household and still they had not reached the port. A landslide had blocked the road and, in the effort to traverse the track they had only partly managed to clear, a wagon had broken a wheel. The night was fast approaching and it was becoming unsafe to continue. He knew he must call a stop and hope the convoy was not being followed. He knew it was dangerous but could see his convoy members were exhausted and needed rest. He ordered the wagons to find a safe place away from the track. Fires would be allowed just long enough to cook the food; they would have to sleep cold tonight. As he walked through the camp he gazed at the children huddled together to gather any warmth possible. He thought how much Cassian took upon himself when he chose to care for these people. Most men in his position would not have cared for those that serve them but Cassian was different, sinking his emotions into the well-being of his slaves. He was at a loss as to why Cassian did such a thing, Lucius looked at his hands. They were shaking, not from the cold but because of the fear and weight of being responsible for each of these souls. He walked from the camp until he came to rest high on a ridge which overlooked the surrounding countryside. Sleep would not visit him tonight. He would gaze to the horizon and watch for danger and he promised himself he would never again accept such a mission.

Flabinus consumed a large goblet of wine and then called his scouts to him.

'The hunt is on, our prey is clever and resourceful and so we must match him. Cassian has business interests around most of the known world and therefore we must find his destination. He would not have liked to be on the road too long, this would have left him vulnerable with women and children to defend. Therefore his options are limited. I believe he will head to one of four ports.' As he spoke he pointed to differing locations on a map before him.

'Have you got any idea which of the convoy he travels in?' One of the scouts asked, while trying not to raise Flabinus' anger.

'I have an idea but it matters not. Ultimately both convoys will lead to the same place. Cassian will try to throw a protective arm around all of his household, this will be his undoing. You will divide into four groups and go to these ports. You will find out from where they travelled and on which vessel. Find out their destination by any means necessary.'

'And if we come across them?'

'You will not, Cassian is not a fool. He will want to choose his battleground, a place where he believes he can protect his people. So you will gather information only. Do I make myself clear?'

The scouts nodded their agreement and were gone in a moment; they had learnt that when Flabinus gave an order it was a good idea to react quickly and without hesitation. Flabinus smiled to himself, a particularly demonic smile. He so loved the chase. He always felt like a particularly intelligent cat playing with an ignorant mouse, so ignorant that it never saw the bigger picture - one in which no matter how many times it sensed freedom was just about to be won, the large paw would sweep down and pin it to the ground. He wondered if Cassian would be a decent challenge rather than the pointless rodents he had eradicated lately. He had heard talk of the man, hopefully the chase would be a little more interesting than usual, so often he was left numb by the tedium of it all.

Lathyrus had removed Cassian and his group from the docks with no problems; he had been surprised by the anxiety on his friend's face which refused to relax until the vessel started out to sea. Many of the group settled down to sleep, even the unsettling motion of the waves seemingly having no affect upon them or delaying their slumber. Few had enjoyed much sleep on land, each movement and noise in the dark making them jump expecting an assassin to emerge from the darkness. Lathyrus observed the tell tales signs of sleep deprivation upon all their faces and his concern grew. Whatever troubles could affect such a man as Spartacus must be grave indeed. He wanted to ask Cassian what was going on but, on seeing the man up close, Lathyrus demanded he went to get some rest. At first Cassian began to argue but Lathyrus pointed out there was only one captain aboard, the young Roman finally relented and, as he left, he gently patted Lathyrus on the shoulder to show he understood and appreciated the concern the old sea dog had shown for him.

The voyage would take time; Spartacus once again discovered his loathing for the sea had not abated. The cramped conditions only served to intensify his bad mood, even thoughts of his wife did nothing to shake him from his darkness. Spartacus was worried. He had hoped he and his family would be allowed to live out their days in peace; instead once again he must prepare to do battle and protect those he loved. He wondered whether he should have taken his family away when Cassian had told him of the impending danger, inwardly chastising himself for always having to be honourable. Many men would have gladly turned and walked away from the situation, especially with the coin and the means to reach any dark little shadow in the known world and slip quietly from view. He decided that's what he should have done but, as he came to the conclusion, he felt ashamed at even contemplating it.

'Damn it!' he cursed, although it was not aimed at anyone particularly, more a curse to himself. Aegis rested himself next to Spartacus and looked at the powerful warrior.

'You, I think, are not built for sea travel,' he said, a gentle smile upon his face.

'It makes my guts turn over,' Spartacus replied.

'And your mind I see. You should not torment yourself.'

'Aegis, I have been fighting all my life and for what? Still my family are threatened.'

'But your wife and daughter are here Spartacus, they are at your side and when they look at you there are no recriminations. They love and respect the man you are.'

Spartacus blushed slightly, never comfortable with such intimate compliments. He had heard the crowds of many arenas screaming their love for him as a warrior on the sand, but that was somehow dishonest. He always knew that if the next warrior who faced him was victorious then the crowd would cheer just as loud. Aegis though was a friend, but unlike any he had ever experienced before. He did not massage your ego or dress up his comments so

61

that it would not cause hurt, he commented as he saw and as he felt.

'Between yourself and Cassian, I feel we will survive.'

'I wish I could be as sure.'

'Oh I'm not sure Spartacus, it's just I can't afford to lose any more limbs. I struggle to wipe my arse as it is.'

Spartacus and Aegis erupted into laughter, and the first drops of rain began to collide with the deck.

Lathyrus stood at the tiller like a proud Colossus. The rain and wind whipped at him. Each gust was met curses from the big man, as he refused to yield to nature's ferocious attempt to drag him from the deck. The screams of his passengers and crew reached fever pitch as all feared the vessel would be torn apart and all aboard would be dragged to a watery oblivion. The boat had begun to take on too much of the sea and many of the passengers had climbed onto the deck, fearing being trapped beneath deck if the craft did falter and let the waves take her. Spartacus glanced to the port side and fear took him as a huge wave was hurtling towards them him. He cried out his warning, at the same time grasping his family close, bracing his powerful limbs to withstand nature's onslaught. In his mind he already knew his attempts were futile as, because no matter how powerful the man, the forces of the God's could tear this craft apart in a blink of an eye. Lathyrus worked wonders; he could not avoid the wave but managed to turn the boat so it would receive as little impact as possible from the ever looming menace. Despite the impact being reduced as the wave struck it drove the air from Spartacus's body but he clung to his family. He chanced a look up from those he loved and his eyes were met with horror as Druro's son was ripped from his father's arms. The world slowed and entered an almost spectral plain as Spartacus observed the screaming boy reaching out his hands in search of his father; his attempts were in vain. Another wave stuck and the force of it twisted the boy into the air and, in a moment, he was gone. Wave after wave struck the craft but somehow the knowledge and skill of Lathyrus prevented it from disappearing into the depths. With the rain still lashing down stinging any exposed flesh the crew and vessel limped from the storm.

Gradually passengers moved, releasing their talon like grips and dared to tend the wounded and petrified. Druro didn't speak, he merely sought solitude removing himself from the deck. Epionne watched him go, tears mixing with the salted rain upon her face.

'Can we reach our destination?' Cassian screamed to Lathyrus, the wind still making communication difficult.

'Not in this condition, we will need to make repairs.' Lathyrus boomed back.

'We need to keep to our schedule.'

'Then you had best start giving orders to the seas, for they are not listening to your plans.' His words were harshly spoken for he had watched some of his crew die today and Cassian's plans were of little importance to him. Epionne was tending her sons when Druro approached carrying documents which he had obviously obtained from beneath deck.

'Cassian will have need of these.' He spoke quietly, forcing Epionne to strain to hear his words.

'What do you mean?' But the man never answered, he simply turned and walked away from her. Meanwhile Cassian had seen the annoyance rise in Lathyrus' face and sought to make amends.

'Forgive me my friend, I speak without thought.' His words were not answered for a terrible scream split the air.

'No Druro! No!' Epionne had issued the scream as she finally realised the man's intentions. All the vessel's inhabitants turned to stare at Druro as he stepped over the rail and, with just one glance over his shoulder which showed to all his sadness and resignation, he calmly stepped over the side. Spartacus raced to the side but Druro had vanished quickly below the waves, heartily welcomed to the bosom of the sea. Even so Spartacus called for him, desperately searching for a sign that he may still live and be plucked from oblivion. Druro had chosen to join his son, the adventure they would share would take place in the afterlife.

The craft, beaten and smashed, limped towards a small island. The land was ringed by ferocious rocks and to all those who did not possess a certain knowledge. The island guarded its inland, with few being allowed hospitality. Lathyrus however, was one of the few men alive who did know its secrets and slowly, and with anxiety growing aboard the ship, he picked his way through the dagger-like rocks which waited, poised to tear the bottom from any careless ship. Eventually they reached a small cove and, before long, the passengers were spilling onto the beach, glad to be rid of the sea and her perils. The children who had suffered on the journey showed amazing spirit, laughing and playing in the sand and this more than anything else seemed to mobilise the rest of the group. The men set to making a camp which would shelter them and enable food to be prepared. In the morning repairs would be started but for now all needed to rest, and try to forget the image of Druro stepping to oblivion.

The night wore on and eventually the rain stopped. The high rocky walls of the cove protected the camp from the sharp wind. Fires were lit and food prepared, the nourishment warmed the souls and many even felt compelled to sing. Cassian moved away from the group to study the documents Druro had left him, and was soon joined by Spartacus and Lathyrus.

'Well what did he leave us?' Spartacus asked.

You would not believe it if I told you,' his head shaking in amazement, as his eyes scanned the documents.

'What is it?'

'These documents give us a very detailed insight, more or less every aspect of the dealings of our friend Crassus.'

'What use is that to us now?'

'You don't understand. These are high level operations, where vast amounts of coin are being obtained and, perhaps more importantly, everything we need to know about Flabinus.'

It seems Druro had been planning to leave the employ of Crassus for some time.' Lathyrus added.

'Not necessarily. Do you not think I have such a document on those from whom I take orders?' Spartacus skirted over the subject of Cassian's master, for Cassian had promised to give Spartacus his name. However Spartacus's wife had told him not to ask for it and to forget thoughts of revenge for they should concentrate on the living. Spartacus had tried to deny his animal instinct but when conversation came close to his son's killer's identity then the beast awakened within him, pacing its cage, snarling its unrest.

'So what does it say of this Flabinus?' he said quickly, wanting to focus on other matters.

'It gives us an insight of the man himself.'

'We already know, he's a murderous bastard.'

Cassian rolled his eyes to the sky,

'Very well it tells of his weakness and strengths. It also details his home and what's important to him. To be honest, despite my best efforts and that of my agents, I have not been able to find out any information on the man. These documents may provide the weapons we need.'

'Such as?' Spartacus pressed.

'I'm not sure yet, but I do know the information here may well save us all.'

Lathyrus interrupted,

'Then I suggest you study them Cassian and, by the way, my sword, men and life will not leave your side until this matter is settled.' Lathyrus had a look of a man who would not be moved in the matter. Cassian thought for a moment weighing up the advantage of more men, against losing the chance of a quick getaway that Lathyrus and his ship offered.

'Very well, I am honoured that you will be at my side Lathyrus.'

'Ah we will see how long you feel that way.' Lathyrus laughed.

Chapter V

Flabinus and his men had quickly found the intended destination of Cassian and his group; it was amazing how quickly coin and blade loosened a man's tongue. They moved with speed, acquiring some of the fastest vessels which operated on the seas. Flabinus had guessed that if the two convoys had met with even slight delays he may be able to beat them to their destination. Each man carried their own provisions and so could travel light and only those men with the quickest mounts were selected for the initial journey. The rest would follow and hope all the booty would not be taken. Flabinus was possessed, sensing the blood of an enemy. His men stayed clear of him in times like these, knowing his craving could easily spill into aggression aimed at them. They rode, sailed and rode again with devastating pace. The hunt was on and Flabinus could feel his prey slowing, becoming vulnerable and making those small errors which at the time seemed insignificant but which would eventually lead to their downfall. His scouts had told him of an unused fortress, centuries old which stood at the very limits of Cassian's lands. A perfect defensive position with enough men and provisions it would be difficult to prise the defenders from the place and Crassus had already sent word that the matter was taking too long. Just the thought of it made Flabinus push his steed harder and his men responded likewise.

Lucius was pleased; despite being delayed by the weather and bloody stupid Roman administration finally the fortress was in sight. Men, women and children were exhausted, the journey taking every last effort to complete. They climbed the steep dirt track which led to the fortresses heavy wooden doors, each step sapping what remained of their strength. All dreamed of a soft place to lay their head without the dread of more travelling the following day. Even the armed men Cassian had dispatched with the group had removed their armour for to die of exhaustion from the weight of the protective clothing would be of little use to those they guarded. A young child stumbled next to Lucius; he bent his aching body and lifted the child into his arms. It was not a usual act, Lucius usually stayed at arms distance from the other slaves, it made it easier to give orders that way. However with the journey at its end the delight made him forget his usual stuffiness and couldn't help smiling at the young girl. The convoy climbed the twisting track and, after what seemed a lifetime, they finally entered the old fortress, a couple of the guards pushing the heavy doors open. The interior was dusty and it seemed the place had not felt a human touch for many decades. Lucius did not care, before long he and his people would soon have the building habitable. They filed into the main courtyard, relief on their faces. Some slumped to the floor while others smiled and hugged one another.

Lucius smiled and glanced to the skies, happy that the warmth of the sun caressed his aching limbs. The shadow appeared up high and for a moment the glare of the sun prevented recognition but gradually his sight returned and a deep rumble of fear settled in the pit of his stomach. The women and children began to cry and scream as more and more men appeared on the walls above them and around the perimeter of the courtyard. A figure stepped forward, a maniacal mask upon his face. He uttered no words, merely waved his hands and the black cloud descended upon the slaves. Blades rose and fell, the steel did not care for the age or sex of its victim all it craved was blood. When the deed was done, and the beasts were content with the carnage they had created, all followed their leader from the place. No look back was afforded to the fallen or a thought of pity, for these bringers of fear knew only destruction and death, and were devoid of such feelings. They had left their message for Cassian. Now they would retire and when the message had worked in its intended way and destroyed all the hope of their next victims, they would return and the world would run red once again.

Cassian was worried; he had received no news from Lucius. He had learned his charge hand's convoy had landed two days previously but since then nobody had seen the man. All the warriors fixed their armour sensing the unease in their friend. Scouts were placed to warn of any attack and the second convoy began its journey to the fortress.

'How far is it to the fortress?' Lathyrus asked.

'Not far, we should make good time,' replied Cassian, but he seemed far away within realms of his mind. He stayed that way for some time until Aegis returned from scouting with news,

'Four men dressed all in black, watch the fortress.'

'You are sure they just watch the fortress?' asked Cassian.

'Positive, and they are alone.'

Cassian smiled, that must mean they are scouting for Flabinus and haven't entered the fortress yet, the words ticking over in his mind, not spoken out loud.

'Lucius must know they are there, he's keeping his head down,' Spartacus pointed out.

'What do you want me to do with our dark clad friends?' Aegis asked, though he knew what must be done.

'Make it quick and quiet, don't let any slip by you.'

Aegis just nodded his agreement and turned to leave, Bull and Plinius went with him. Spartacus looked at Cassian, a question had been burning inside of him for quite some time,

'Your patron, has he not offered any help?' Cassian was surprised that Spartacus had raised a conversation that involved his master.

'He said he will help where he can, but to a certain extent his hands were tied as Flabinus operated in the back alleys of Rome and the senate, but he would use all his influence to prevent Flabinus carrying out his mission.'

'Sounds like he's washing his hands of us.'

'Possibly, but I would be surprised. The man usually stands by his men as long as it doesn't compromise his position in Rome.'

'And we wouldn't want that would we?'

Cassian smiled, he knew because of circumstances Spartacus would never see his master in a good light and did not blame him.

73

His master gave the order which took the life of Spartacus's son. It worried Cassian what would happen if the day ever came when Spartacus and his master should meet. An involuntary shudder shook his body for that would be a bloody day. Cassian looked to the skies and the sun was already beginning to set. It seemed quiet, almost too quiet even the birds in the trees gave the impression of being mute. He could see the fortress looming though no inhabitants showed themselves. This was not surprising, he knew Lucius would have all of his people hiding away, attempting to show any onlookers that the ancient building was empty of all life. Aegis and the others returned and, with a simple nod, told Cassian the task had been completed without any problem and so the convoy trundled on to its place of rest.

Now the fortress bore down upon them and Cassian nodded to Aegis to check it out before the rest passed through the huge heavy wooden doors. Though closed the doors were not bolted and the large man slipped through the entrance and into the interior.

'I think a decent meal is in order Spartacus, this area used to be rich with wild boar.' said Cassian.

'I agree-' began Spartacus, but the rest of his words were lost as Aegis slipped back through the gate and slumped to the ground.

The group watched in dismay as the huge man wept. Cassian's entire body stiffened,

'Plinius, be so kind as to guard the convoy. I am sorry Spartacus if you could accompany me inside.'

Spartacus nodded in agreement though he feared what awaited him. Cassian only opened the heavy doors enough for Spartacus and himself to enter, not wanting the women and children to observe what lay within. He braced himself, steeled his heart to guard against the terror which his eyes would have to endure. It didn't work, before him lay carnage. Men, women and children slaughtered in a manner that most would not have believed possible to be carried out by human beings. Tears streamed from his eyes, he knew these people. He glanced around his eyes falling on the faces of the children, he lost all the Roman resolve he had tried so long to perfect, it melted away with each horrific sight. Spartacus too could not hide the effects of the slaughter and tears rolled freely from his eyes. He found the body of Lucius which had been stabbed and slashed to almost complete destruction. His remains were still hunched over that of a young child in a forlorn hope to try and protect her from the enemies that killed without mercy. Spartacus wiped the blood from the small girl's face, such a pretty girl he thought to himself trying to block out the vista of the surrounding area. A tear dropped from the tip of his nose and landed on the girl's cheek. An involuntary flinch took Spartacus by surprise. He bent down close, and saw the girl was holding her breath. Clearly she had been given instruction by Lucius to play dead and not to open her eyes, no matter what she heard. The huge gladiator carefully lifted the girl as though she was made of smoke and would simply drift away. As he did so she began to cry, obviously terrified of what might happen,

'Sshh, my beautiful little girl you are safe now, keep your eyes closed tight until I say, understand?' The girl nodded in compliance and, though still whimpering, she held so tightly to Spartacus as if she feared he would put her back amongst the horror. He slipped past the doors once more. Flora stood before him and without saying a word he placed the child in her arms. Flora took the child,

'Who's a beautiful little flower? Let's get you cleaned up.' The child never spoke but willingly went with Flora. Spartacus returned inside to see Cassian already clearing the bodies away.

'Shall I call more men?'

76

'No they must stay outside and guard the women and children, if you would be so kind as to help me.' Spartacus was sure that protecting the women wasn't the only reason, any person seeing this carnage could not help it affecting their confidence and moral. Cassian was clearly trying to prevent what was left of his household becoming despondent for they would need all their spirit when Flabinus returned.

'Why do you think he left?' Spartacus asked, more to isolate his mind from the horror of which his eyes presented him with at each turn.

'Like I said before, Flabinus is no simple assassin he likes to toy with his victims before he visits death upon them. He knows what such an act will have on our fighting spirit. He has also cut our defensive capabilities down by nearly half with the men he slaughtered here, this man believes we are beaten.'

'Then he is mistaken.'

Cassian looked at the warrior at his side, he couldn't help feel such admiration for the man. He had endured such terrible hardship in his life and yet he still refused to bend his knee to the fates. His skill with a sword was matched by his bravery but, even more importantly, it was matched by the honour with which he tried to live.

'So what's our next move?'

'Firstly we make this place as fortified as possible, then we find out exactly where Flabinus resides, because it's about time we started giving the man more to think about.'

'Well it's taken you long enough.' said Spartacus, slightly sharper than he intended.

'What has?' Cassian replied, confused by the warrior's response.

'Cassian, the men you have at your command are not used to sitting and waiting for death.   They, and I include you in this, are warriors and are better employed in taking the fight to an enemy no matter how disadvantageous the odds.'

'That's all well and good Spartacus, but with have our families to consider.'

'There are more ways to take the battle to Flabinus than simply marching out and meeting his army.'

'What do you have in mind?'

'First let us finish here and get the convoy within the safety of the walls, but I suggest we visit some horror on the bastard responsible for this.' His eyes moved to the faces of the fallen, pale like milk and twisted from the agony they had suffered. 'The voices of these poor wretched souls cry out from beyond the grave Cassian, we must avenge this evil no matter what the cost.'

'No matter the cost,' Cassian repeated and nodded his agreement.

It was dark before all the bodies had been placed upon a cart and driven from the fortress. Cassian himself lit the torch which would hide the physical disgrace Flabinus had carried out. Though the bodies burned the memory of what Flabinus had done burned hotter than any earthly fire could create. Flabinus had wanted to destroy the moral of these men but, in truth, he had joined each of them together with a bond so tight in could prove impossible to break. His actions had forged a determination in the men which would only cease when Flabinus and those who served him were lying broken upon the ground. The night wore on and, as the children settled into their new beds, the women fretted on what had happened within the fortress. Spartacus understood their worries but finally lost his temper,

'Listen we have no choice but to be here, there's no point worrying about what might happen. Come the morning we will start to fortify this place and Flabinus will need an army to get in here. Beside before long that bastard will have his own worries.'

The outburst had shocked the women into silence, Spartacus was usually the sullen one of the group only really showing happiness as he played with his family. The words he spoke had an impact, for so long they had heard how they must run and fear the dreaded Flabinus, the mere mention of his name had started to bring fear upon its uttering. Spartacus had challenged this fear, he would fight this man and his hordes and believed totally he would be victorious. A kind of peace had settled over the group for the first time since arriving at the fortress, a small difference in each of their hearts had been sparked from Spartacus's speech. The difference was hope, for when Spartacus was angry there was always hope.

Flora settled the young girl down, she had washed all the blood from her fragile form. Her clothes however were given to Tictus and he was given instruction they should be burned. Flora had been most implicit and insistent on the matter, as though burning the rags would somehow eradicate the horrors the girl had endured. Flora had always craved a daughter but the Gods had seen fit not to bestow her home with one. Deep down, as she cared for the young girl, she vowed that she would take the child as her own. She caressed the child's hair and sang a soothing melody hoping the tenderness of her actions would chase away the nightmares which would try to visit the mind of one far too young to understand them.

Chapter VI

The night passed with the occupants of the old fortress all keen to see the rising of the sun. Though most of the men were not on duty still they watched from the walls, not wanting to rely solely on the sentries which had been posted. Cassian, Spartacus, Aegis, Plinius and Tictus planned how best disrupt the plans of Flabinus, while Bull, Lathyrus and Crannicus continually went over the defences, eager to eradicate any opportunities for the enemy. It was a strange night where any sound emanating from the wilderness beyond the walls was met with the scraping of swords as the defenders readied themselves. Spartacus saw the nerves etched on the faces of each of the inhabitants and cursed Flabinus for his tactics of striking fear into his enemies was having success. Spartacus vowed to himself that the next day he would spread a little fear of his own, and maybe grate the nerves of that bastard assassin. He remembered the first Roman legions sent to round up his slave army; raw, untested soldiers who thought they faced just a rabble. As the nights passed and the soldiers began to die in the darkness the confidence of those Romans had melted away with each rising of the sun. The battle was short and bloody, the legion evaporating before the slave army, its will to fight worn down by the previous night's carnage. They had not seen or heard the enemy which had swooped down upon them in the night but still their comrades died, and when the morning light shone down and highlighted the blood soaked ground. The looks of terror still etched upon the faces of the fallen, fear had gripped the soldiers of Rome.

Eventually light bathed the fortress, bringing with it a sense of relief which could almost be tasted on the air. It was unlikely Flabinus could launch a sneak attack in the daytime, the fortress had been placed well all those centuries ago. It dominated the countryside and left an attacker little option but to come straight up the steep winding track which lead to its main entrance. The defenders would be afforded the luxury of ample warning and would be able to rain down missiles on their attackers. Although Flabinus had numbers on his side, a full scale frontal attack would see most of those numbers perish or at least be wounded. For now the defenders were safe. Only the returning, unstoppable darkness would bring back the shadow of fear, which would lurk behind each noise that shook the night air.

Aegis had done his work with skill, he had plotted the location of Flabinus' camp, or as it turned out three camps. Their enemy was cautious, he had based two smaller camps closer in proximity to the fortress so he would be warned if any attacks were to take place. Cautious and in no rush it seemed, for although he set his sentries he made no move towards the fortress. Spartacus guessed Flabinus wanted the atrocity he had carried out to have time to do its work, grating on the nerves of those who sought refuge beyond the tall, ancient stone walls of the fortress. Spartacus smiled to himself, he had made a vow and this day would see the beginnings of that vow bear fruit. Today the enemy would bleed, but for now the new day continued as the previous had ended. Defences were improved and provisions were gathered from the surrounding countryside. With each stone placed on the wall and each weapon sharpened the confidence of the inhabitants seemed to grow. Though Spartacus was pleased to observe the transformation he knew it was still a fragile confidence, one which needed to be protected and nurtured.

All too soon the sun began to dip below the far mountains and, as it did, Spartacus and Plinius emerged from the makeshift armoury. Both carried extra weapons for the task which lay ahead of them. Their faces were like stone as they required complete concentration upon the deeds they must fulfil. Loved ones were merely afforded a polite nod for this was not the time to think on family, only the destruction of the enemy could be given space within the mind. The two slipped from the fortress, becoming one with the shadows which grew tall with the falling sun. Spartacus led Plinius to where Aegis observed the first of the enemy camps. As they approached Aegis acknowledged them with a slight nod of his head, but his gaze never left his prey.

'They are getting comfortable,' he said, handing Spartacus a skin of wine.

'Well we wouldn't want them to get bored. Let's see if we can stir them up a bit.'

The three waited until the sun had completely disappeared and then began to pick their way towards the unsuspecting foe. Plinius was amazed at himself; no nerves or dread, he questioned himself whether that was good or bad thing. He remembered Spartacus telling him that fear and nerves kept a man's edge, without them a man became sloppy and liable to make mistakes. He wondered whether or not it was possible to make yourself feel nervous. Spartacus raised his hand, they stood just a few paces from the first guard. He leant against a large spear, his head lolling as he fought the dreams which wished to take him. The flash of Spartacus' dagger took his throat out, the chance to scream and alert his comrades too brief and fleeting. A second and third guard fell similarly, without as much as a questioning grunt emanating from the camp. The way was now clear, approximately thirty men were at slumber. That was far too many to slaughter quietly so the three warriors picked their targets and moved ghost like through the camp. Men died quickly, their attackers moving rapidly and silently to the next victim. By the time Spartacus signalled for his comrades to leave the camp twelve men had breathed their last, their final desperate breaths taken from them by thieves in the night. Spartacus waited until they had retired a safe distance then slapped both Aegis and Plinius on the shoulder for a job well done. He whispered to Aegis,

'Hide yourself well my friend, for I fear they will look hard come the morning.'

'Fear for me not Spartacus, those men are used to hiding in the shadows not searching them.'

Both Spartacus and Plinius had travelled a good distance and were looking forward to rest by the time the first cries of alarm split the silence in the enemy's camp. They initially came from one of the younger assassins, who kicked his sleeping comrade next to him. The man who he believed in slumber was known as Tux and he had a tendency, after a night on the wine, to urinate whilst asleep. The young assassin had been pissed on in the night one too many nights for his liking. The liquid had soaked into his clothes and, despite not wanting to wake himself, he forced a kick at his neighbour. When finally he gave up trying to rouse him and rose unwillingly, he glanced at Tux. His sleep blurred vision cleared only for horror to meet his eyes, the sight forcing bile to rise in his throat which prevented the scream he yearned to make. He struggled from his tent, vomiting freely on to the ground. When finally, his guts had no more to offer he screamed the alarm. At first he was met with little more than grunts but then, as the other men were forced awake and were greeted with similar sights of carnage, the camp exploded into activity. Aegis watched from his vantage point and spoke quietly to himself,

'Not quite so much fun now is it?' A smile spread upon his face, it had not been an enjoyable task to slaughter men in this way, but a slaughter they deserved.

By midday within the fortress Cassian closed on Spartacus. He had not asked for news when the huge warrior had returned, preferring instead to let the man rest, but now Spartacus had risen it was important he knew how the previous night's activities had gone.

'It was a successful night?'

'At least a dozen will trouble us no more,' Spartacus replied.

'Will he come now, do you think?'

'I don't profess to know the man, but I think he will wait and see if he has any more visitors this night. I doubt he cares too deeply for the men he has lost,' replied Spartacus.

'Well he can wait, I have no wish to lose you my friend.'

'Oh we are going back.'

'What?' Cassian replied, exasperated.

'Think about it Cassian! To lose men to a surprise raid is one thing but to lose men when you are waiting for them, that will truly send fear amongst their ranks. We will have it so the poor buggers won't dare close their eyes, fearing the cold rasp of a blade upon their throats.'

'You speak from experience?'

'Yes I have experienced both sides, neither is pleasant. When I was just a boy in the auxiliaries we were sent out to hunt some local bandit and his followers, only the bastard didn't know he was supposed to be some local village idiot. He led us a merry dance, in the day we chased our tails and in the night we died. They came from the shadows, sometimes just one soldier would die, but on other nights five or six would be found bleeding in the dirt.'

'What happened?' Cassian asked, eager to hear the bandit had met his end.

'When finally our numbers had fallen to almost half we retreated. Though to say retreat does not really do it justice. I ran so fast I nearly wore my sandals away.Fuck! I was scared.'

'And what of the bandit?'

'Probably still up in those hills, I know no more patrols were sent up. Besides he earnt his freedom.'

The fortress began to bathe in the dimming light of the setting sun once again. Word of the exploits of Spartacus and Plinius the night before had spread throughout its inhabitants. A new confidence began to emanate from those within, also many seemed to think justice had been served. Spartacus and Plinius once again slipped from the fortress, picking their way to the meeting point

89

with Aegis. They joined him as he lay on a small hillock observing the camp below,

'They have been busy,' he whispered, nodding in the camp's direction.

'You clapped eyes on that bastard Flabinus?' Plinius asked.

'No, seems he likes messengers to do the leg work.'

'So tell me,' Spartacus interrupted, 'what's he been up to?'

'They have doubled the guards and set up a few nasty little surprises for anyone who approaches unannounced.'

'And the second camp?'

'The same but all the traps and extra guards are on this side of the camp. Bloody poor preparation that's all I can say.'

'Right then our path is clear, but first I need to tell you something. The time for simply killing these bastards has passed. We need to force Flabinus' hand if we are to make him act rashly. We need to send a message to those men down there that will make them fear us more than they fear Flabinus.'

'What do you have in mind?' Plinius asked, though he wondered how they could be more impressive than the night before. Spartacus went on to explain his plan, with each detail both Plinius and Aegis stared in disbelief. Not only at the task that lay ahead but also the acts which they must do, for both saw themselves as warriors and, when possible, men of honour.

Darkness covered the camps, though the three men who approached the second camp noticed the fires had been piled that little bit higher this night. They worked their way around the second camp, approaching from the opposite side to which they had attacked the previous night. Spartacus nodded and the three moved into the camp. The guards fell quickly and quietly on that side, obviously they had felt secure they guarded an area away from the enemy. This assumption had sealed their fate and those of many of their sleeping comrades, who opened their eyes only seconds before Charon held out his hand for payment to cross into the next world. The three climbed the small hillock which would afford them the safety to rest. They glanced at each other, their shame evident upon their faces. Each carried a bag filled to spilling point and bulging at the sides. Spartacus looked down at the bags and then at his two friends. Even in the darkness he could tell they were covered in blood, the smell of which was beginning to make him gag.

'You two head back to the fortress. Come the morning they will search this area, leaving no stones unturned.'

91

'And you?' Aegis enquired.

'I will sort these bags out and join you shortly.'

The morning broke, the sun already storming the walls of the light cloud cover above, all the world seemed at peace. The guard from the first camp wandered over to his friend who had been placed on duty at the edge of the second camp. With a clear sound of relief he spoke to his fellow guard,

'Quiet night, thank the Gods.'

'Same here, haven't heard a thing for hours.'

'Must be about breakfast time.' A strange look appeared over his friends face as he spoke, 'What's wrong?'

'Like I said I haven't heard a thing. Absolutely nothing!' The two broke into a run until they reached the camp. Though they could see only tents and no visible signs of trouble they could feel a terrible sense of foreboding. It was not long before Flabinus was striding through the camp, each tent he visited was the same. The bodies lay drenched in thick crimson blood, there were no signs of battle, merely butchery. The flesh was pale for the loss of blood had been immense, the removal of the head had a tendency to be messy as the arteries gave way to the blade. He exploded, his wrath falling upon the guards of the second camp, whom he dispatched with his own hands. He ordered his entire army to search the countryside, but he knew their foe had slipped away in the darkness and would not be found. Then at the edge of a clearing his scouts did find something which they reported to Flabinus immediately. He rode out at once to the site and there the heads of his men adorned wooden shafts. The confident Flabinus felt a chill race down his spine and for the first time he experienced the icy spectre of not being in control. He clenched his fist until the knuckles turned chalk white. Confusion raced through him and mingled with indignation. His prey were beginning to annoy him, this was not how they were supposed to behave, they were supposed to shrink with fear as he took all from them, before finally taking their life. He chanced a sideways glance at the faces of his own men and could clearly see the concern that he was so used to seeing in his enemy. He turned his horse and made to ride away,

'Sir, shouldn't we bury them?'

'Whatever for? They have failed in their duties and I have no time for such men. Let the carrion feast upon them.' Flabinus noticed the disgust in the young man's face. 'That bothers you?'

The warrior took an involuntary step backwards as he became aware of the danger he now found himself in,

'No sir,' he dared not look at the man before him as he spoke.

'Good mount up, or you will never leave this place.'

Chapter VII

By the time Spartacus returned to the fortress the sun was already beating strongly upon the ancient masonry of the fort He had taken his time to observe how his actions had affected the men of Flabinus, he smiled at their reaction. Though he really wished to have been able to see the man himself in detail, he had never obtained more than a brief glimpse of him. He slipped inside the heavy wooden doors and Cassian stood observing the state of him. Virtually his entire body was covered in dried blood,

'Are you injured?'

'It's not mine, I'm fine. Did Plinius and Aegis get back alright?'

'I believe so, although I haven't spoken to them,' replied Cassian.

'Pull the scouts back inside the fortress. He will come today. Make all the preparations, but nobody sets foot outside the fortress.'

Cassian didn't question the order, but simply began barking out his own orders to all. In a way he was glad, Flabinus had been forced

95

to act by the actions of Spartacus. There would be no long, agonising wait for an attack. They would put Flabinus to the test and, as Cassian looked at Spartacus, he almost felt sorry for the enemy, for Spartacus took on the vision of Hades itself when the war horn sounded.

Flabinus was angry and in no mood for his men to react slowly to his orders. His fist connected with the jaw of one of those who moved too slowly. He called for Strixus, a man greater in years than most in Flabinus' army, who took great care to approach his master warily,

'You called for me Flabinus,' the old man spoke cautiously.

'I want two siege weapons; we must be able to get the men to those walls in good order.'

'It will take time.'

'You have two days and all the men you wish, we have numbers on our side. I wish it to remain that way when the hand to hand fighting starts. Flabinus wanted to attack that very night, but knew that the old fortress would cause the loss of too many men.

'It will be done.' Strixus moved away quickly wishing to place as much distance between himself and his dangerous master.

Flabinus watched the man go. He would have liked to assault the walls of that fortress immediately, but knew it would result in heavy losses. Losing men was not overly concerning to him; he had plenty who could replace them. However he had read the reports of his enemy's skill with the blade, and wished to ensure victory. To do that he would require as many fighting men as possible, for he knew Cassian and his followers would not die easily, and he so wanted them to die.

The preparations went well, there was plenty of food and the old well had been cleared of debris revealing an ample supply of fresh water. Cassian was in his element; he looked at all the possible issues and made plans to counteract them. If there could be a whirlwind of administration he would be it. Bull did his best to keep up the spirits of those around him, laughing and joking with the non-combatants. Spartacus had thought to chastise the man, but saw the positive effect he was having upon all in the fortress. Plinius took time to show Chia how to use a sword and Aegis instructed Crannicus how to use a bow. The man was out of shape and would not be adequate in hand to hand fighting but he could still kill at a distance as well as any other. Rocks were carried up to the highest part of the walls, they could be hurled down upon the enemy and, by some amazing stroke of luck, Tictus had stumbled across an old store room filled with ancient weapons. They would be virtually useless for fighting with, hence the reason they had not been pillaged over the years, but as missiles they would be deadly. They toiled away for hours until a warning call went up from the wall. Spartacus and Cassian raced to the ramparts eager to see an enemy, wanting their destruction.

Dust rose in the distance, it obscured any chance of observing the advancing enemy. All mounted on the wall were straining their eyes to catch the first glimpse of the enemy. Then, drifting upon the gentle wind, came the sound of marching men. The steady thumping of leather sandals and the tell-tale scrape of metal studs hitting the ground in unison, Bull whooped,

'No assassins march in order, that's the legion.'

The confused Spartacus glanced at Cassian,

'But how? I thought we were on our own.'

'Evidently things have changed,' replied Cassian.

The sound intensified and then gradually through the clouds of dust came the armoured fist of the Roman Empire. Onwards they marched, drawing ever closer to the fortress. An involuntary shudder raced down Spartacus' back, he had never grown used to the legions marching towards him. Cassian moved to give the signal to open the gates,

'Wait!' shouted Spartacus. 'It could be a trap.'

Cassian went to argue but his mind hastily remembered the foe they were dealing with and he decided quickly caution was required. So the defenders stood their ground not yielding their vantage spot and waited for the legion to come to them. Eventually the heavy drumming of marching came to an end and a large centurion stepped to the front,

'I am centurion Lintus. I have come on the orders of Gnaeus Pompeius Magnus,' he held up a scroll as proof of his words.

'What are those orders?' Cassian bellowed down.

'Titus Flabinus has been declared an enemy of the Senate. We are to assist you in the destruction of both the man and his men.'

Cassian struggled to keep his joy in check, finally they would be rid of Flabinus. He waved the centurion forward though the legionaries stayed their ground. As the centurion entered the fortress all around eagerly listened to the conversation between him and Cassian. As each word was spoken the relief was palpable within the walls. Some of the women even cried with joy, the stresses of the last few days suddenly being released. Bursting into tears would have been frowned upon if the men had followed the example of the women, so they had to content themselves with blowing out their cheeks with the relief, though the emotions inside were every much as raw as the women's.

The night wore on and the new guests were made comfortable and provided with a decent meal. Bull was in his element, laughing and joking with the soldiers. Plinius too seemed to enjoy the company of their new allies, only Spartacus kept his distance. The relief at reinforcements was soon tainted by the feelings he had for men serving the Empire. As the night came to a close and tired men rested, Cassian called a meeting to decide their next course of action. It was decided that Aegis would once again venture out and scout the enemy position. Cassian would prefer to go on the attack but to do that he must have good information. Aegis left the fortress taking with him a couple of men to act as runners to keep up a constant flow of information between himself and Cassian. When news returned that the enemy were preparing siege weapons it was clear an opportunity had presented itself. The enemy were busy which would give Cassian's forces the chance to strike and crush Flabinus once and for all, and so they made their plans.

The legionaries had been at the fortress for a full day and they proved to be very resourceful. It seemed they could adapt to any surroundings. The fortress was in full flow, temporary forges had been set up and weapons were honed for the upcoming engagement. Cassian strode about the camp with Lintus, both thoroughly checked the preparations while talking of happenings back in Rome. Cassian found out that Pompey had forced the Senate's hand regarding Flabinus, though he dared not link the man publicly with Crassus. Lintus told how Crassus had smiled serenely as the motion was passed, Flabinus his trusted assassin was made an enemy of Rome and it never caused a flicker. Cassian doubted that inside Crassus had been so serene, although he could always find men to do his bidding with the gold the man possessed. Lintus wandered off to scream at some of his men who were becoming a little loud. Cassian spied Bull and motioned for the man to join him,

'Bull I must ask you a favour.'

'Of course, what is it?'

'Tomorrow we go into battle. Both I and Spartacus must go and so I need a man I can trust to look after the families left behind,' as he finished talking he noticed Bull become crestfallen.

He quickly added, 'I realise you would wish to march with the army, but there is no other I would trust with my family.' Bull raised his head,

'Of course, with my life Cassian.'

'Thank you my friend.'

The troops moved out quietly, though the enemy were nowhere to be seen. They would need to move quickly to be in position for the rising of the sun. The plan was to surround the enemy camp, cutting off any hope of escape. They came upon the place where Spartacus had spiked the heads of the enemy, Cassian gagged at the site,

'Very effective.'

'I thought so,' Spartacus replied, though Cassian noticed he did not look once at the horrific display he had created, preferring to look out to where the enemy sentries patrolled unaware of the swords which moved towards them. Each step became lighter upon the ground as they neared the enemy, each snap of a twig seemed to be amplified tenfold. The legionaries fanned out, encircling the enemy and closing a deadly trap. Each man almost stopped breathing knowing the importance of finding their position undetected. The encirclement was complete and now the men rested, they would attack at first light. With the ground so uneven to attack in poor light could break up the assault before it began. So, with lookouts posted, the soldiers lay down and tried to sleep. The more experienced of them slipped away into slumber easily but the younger, more raw soldiers fiddled with weaponry and armour and a number had to be ordered to keep the noise down. Finally the light broke through the darkness and the soldiers began to wake. As if working on instinct they even came from slumber without making a sound. Not far from them the enemy camp was just stirring into activity, however it would be sometime before the majority of them would be awake.

Spartacus was lying down next to Cassian, wondering when the attack was actually going to start. He could tell his Roman friend was nervous, this was a different kind of fighting to the arena, but also knew the aristocrat wished vengeance for those of his household Flabinus had put to death. Then all of a sudden they were moving, slowly at first, with virtually no sound being made, but then the speed intensified and the legionaries roared a beast like scream. The guards fell quickly caught between raising the alarm or running, indecision cost them dear as swords cut them down. Onwards they went, Spartacus taking the throat from an enemy guard who chose to stand and fight. As they reached the camp, already screams were emanating from Flabinus' men. Most were coming from their tents bewildered at what was happening. Legionaries swarmed through the camp, bloody gladius rising and falling and rising again. Few of the defenders put up a meaningful defence; they sought to escape the slaughter by running from the enemy to the front. However, they ran straight into more enemy no matter which way they turned. The carnage was over quickly, the dead and dying littering the ground, the smell of freshly opened bodies clogging the nostrils. Plinius approached Spartacus who had just ended the suffering of man with a quick thrust,

'Have we found Flabinus?' he asked.

'I wouldn't know, don't know the man.'

As Spartacus answered, Cassian approached. Behind him three men were being dragged without ceremony by a number of legionaries. Cassian stopped and the captives were hurled down at his feet, all had slight wounds and the fear could be clearly seen in their eyes. Cassian looked at the men, the loathing etched upon his face,

'I will ask only once, where is the body of Flabinus?'

'You will not find him here.' The oldest of the three spoke, a sword slash to his face had opened part of his face, but it wasn't deep and did not prevent him from speaking.

'Then where?'

'Two days ago he took to sleeping on the hillside,' he gestured towards a close hillside as he spoke. 'He will have seen what has happened and will be on his way to Rome by now.'

Then we must not waste our time here then.' Cassian nodded as he spoke and all three men shrank away from the swords which came for them but there was no possibility of avoiding the blades and they died, shown the type of mercy they had shown their victims.

Spartacus and Cassian surveyed the surrounding hillside. For some time they could see nothing but then Plinius, his younger eyes obviously better for that type of work, pointed out riders in the distance. Cassian observed his enemy escaping,

'Son of a whore!' he swore.

'He's not heading for the port,' Spartacus said, and as realisation dawned upon him, 'he's heading for the fortress.'

'We must go,' Plinius said, the panic starting to rise within him.

'Take off your armour, carry only your weapons,' Spartacus ordered.

Flabinus was on horseback along with approximately twelve men. Cassian and his men were on foot, they had no hope of catching Flabinus, but if they ran until they could run no longer they may reach the fortress before Flabinus had time to plan a way in. They ripped the armour from their bodies and began to run. Lintus would follow with the rest of the men as it would be impossible to keep up the type of pace required with such a large group of men. They hurdled bushes and smashed through snatching tree branches, they tried to force the burning within their lungs out of their minds, the fear of what might happen to their loved ones drove them on. All prayed that Flabinus took his time, secure in the knowledge that his enemy travelled on foot and had no hope of catching him.

Chapter VIII

Crannicus forced the heavy wooden doors open, trying to ignore the protests of the guards at the gate. He looked at the anxious faces of the two men,

'Fine. You two,' he gestured to two further guards who had been watching the proceedings, 'you two can accompany myself and this good lady.'

'But....Bull said nobody was to leave,' the gate guard continued.

'You can say I ordered you to open the gates.'

'You did!'

'Well there you are then, you won't be lying will you?'

The dismayed guard watched the small party leave the fortress and head towards a small hill. He knew there would be trouble when Bull returned to the wall. He thought about sending word immediately but reconsidered seeing no reason to rush into the harsh words he was bound to receive. Sometime later Bull whistled a fine tune, finishing the last of his breakfast he rose and looked to the skies. f all had gone well then the attack may well be over by now and that would be the last the world would see of Flabinus and the dogs he commanded. He climbed the battered stone steps, worn down by the elements and thousands of soldiers' feet. He wondered how many men had fought and died protecting these walls. He acknowledged the guard, for a moment being taken aback by the man's evident anxiety. Reading the glance of the man's eyes beyond the wall Bull quickly followed their direction, looking to the surrounding countryside,

'By the God's! What are they doing outside?'

'Crannicus ordered the gates to be opened.'

'Then why did you not send for me immediately?' Bull's temper was beginning to rise as he spoke.

The guard could not find the words for a reply and forced his eyes downwards to look upon his own feet. He would not and could not meet Bull's stare which was full of ferocity. Bull's fist caught the guard squarely on his jaw, lifting him from his feet and then, unceremoniously, dumping him to the ground.

'Fetch Tictus now!' he bellowed.

The guard raced away, eager to make amends for his failure in his orders and to avoid another blow. Before long Tictus was at Bull's side, dismayed at his father's stupidity,

'I'll go and fetch them.'

'No, we have another problem,' Bull pointed as he spoke. Riders could be clearly seen approaching the small band on the hillside.

'We can't just leave them, what if those riders are Flabinus' men?'

'Give me your sword and listen Tictus, once I am through these gates no matter what happens they do not open again.'

'But…'

'Listen, this fortress has too few to protect it, Cassian ordered we protect the families within these walls, I gave my word. Do I have yours?'

'Yes.' The reply was agonised. Tictus would rather have risked his life to bring back those he loved, much better than watching from afar. Bull did not wait for the young man to change his mind but seized the extra sword, quickly slipped through the gates and ran. He must try to warn Crannicus and his group before the riders came across them.

The small group casually walked amongst the beautiful wild flowers which so effectively decorated the hillside. Crannicus raised a flower to the slender woman by his side,

'Do you think she will like this type?'

'Oh Crannicus that's lovely, Flora will adore it.'

'Thank you so much Epionne, for I have no knowledge in such things. I only know that Flora so misses the tenderness and colours of our villa.'

'She is lucky to have a man who knows her heart so well. Now we must be quick for Cassian will be angry if he knows we have strayed from safety.'

With her words she involuntarily glanced towards the fortress, her eyes becoming fixed upon the running figure. It was some way off but something deep inside made her shiver.

'Crannicus look!'

Crannicus turned to look, but any reply he made was lost as an arrow thudded into the chest of one of the guards, the falling man's scream filling the air. Riders burst into view cutting off any escape route for the small band. The handsome features of their leader somehow becoming grotesque as he glanced down at his fearful prey. The remaining guard and Crannicus drew their swords, with the latter pulling Epionne behind him.

'How very brave. Alas I fear your actions are a pointless gesture. Dismount!' Flabinus drew his sword, 'now I am in need of sport, which of you fine warriors would care to test my blade? Although I have to admit it has been sometime since I fought the likes of you.' He sneered the last of his words and his men laughed, knowing that the match was just about as uneven as a match could be. The guard fell quickly though he did not die with haste. Flabinus took his time delivering blows which would cause as much pain as possible. Then, finally, when the man's fight had left him completely, Flabinus took his head,

'It seems this is the new fashion and I do so like a trophy.' He held the head upon the tip of his sword for all to see. 'Now, fat man, I believe it's your turn.'

Epionne grasped his arm not wanting Crannicus to fight. He looked down into her eyes,

'Forgive me, Epionne. I am a foolish man'

Upon the fortress walls Tictus held Flora close. She wailed her grief knowing that her husband and sister would soon leave this world. She had tried to leave the fortress but Tictus had held firm on his promise, the strength of his arms giving way to tenderness as he felt her will and hope fade. The third cut from Flabinus' blade made a fountain of blood shoot into the air. Crannicus fell to his knees, as he saw the blade rise again he glanced towards the fortress searching the walls for his love. As his eyes met hers there was a further whoosh from the blade and darkness followed, Crannicus was no more. Epionne screamed, the sound was desperate. Flabinus delighted in her misery,

'Now, what to do with you?'

The question could not be answered as a scream went up from one of his men. Flabinus turned to see a blade protruding from the man's chest. Before any could react another man went down and then another. Flabinus grasped Epionne by the hair, pulling her roughly and held a blade to her pearl white throat,

'Excellent! A proper test for my blade.'

'Then leave the woman. Or do you only fight woman and old men?' Bull breathed heavily trying to regain the energy lost in the run. Flabinus casually cast Epionne to one of his men, taking a dagger from his belt. Bull hoped that if he could just keep Flabinus busy, then surely Cassian would return soon. The two circled, Bull with a sword in each hand, matched by Flabinus' holding his sword and dagger. Flabinus was quick but Bull matched him, evading the trickery and speed of the man. Flabinus eventually scored a hit, red liquid poured from Bull's thigh, and then he struck again making a large wound in Bull's forearm.

112

'I must say you are better than my usual opponents, but still lacking the required skill,' Flabinus remarked. As he did he opened up a gash in the chest of Bull. The wounds were sapping his Bull's energy and he knew his time was coming to an end, he spoke privately to himself,

'Just let me make this bastard bleed,' he whispered.
Flabinus darted in to score another hit, this time Bull didn't even try to defend himself, but struck at Flabinus's face. Flabinus howled in agony as Bull's blade raked across the side of his face. He turned in fury at the man who had damaged his precious face, but Bull had sunk to the floor. Flabinus' previous strike had scored a fatal hit, indeed Flabinus' sword was still lodged within Bull's chest. Flabinus bent down close to his opponent,

'All your bravery and still the woman will die. My one regret is you will not see it.'

'Celebrate while you can, for here comes Spartacus,' Bull said managing a weak smile as he whispered.
Flabinus turned to see figures racing towards him, he called for his men to mount. He turned back to Bull but his enemy had already started his last journey. He moved to Epionne,

'I am truly sorry, I would have liked more time with you,' he stroked her hair.

His blade rose quickly, the look of shock replaced the fear in Epionne's eyes, she slumped to the ground. Flabinus casually wiped the blood from his blade on her hair, and mounted his horse. He glanced at the men charging towards him, produced a mock bow and rode away.

Cassian, Spartacus and Plinius reached the forlorn bodies upon the ground. Cassian recognised what remained of Crannicus, while Plinius sobbed over the body of his friend Bull. Spartacus bent down on one knee and turned the slender figure over to reveal her features,

'Cassian my friend, come here.'

Cassian looked over to his friend but the features of the body were obscured to him. However something in the way Spartacus looked at him made an icy hand grasp at his heart. Tictus had finally allowed Flora and the rest to leave the fortress and they came to find their loved ones. They arrived at sadness itself, a terrible scene where Chia tried to soothe Plinius as he held his friend's body close, Flora screamed her grief at the bodies of her husband and sister and Cassian embraced Epionne. Tears cascaded from his eyes, his trembling hands held the bloodied head of his beloved. His heart screamed its agony and beat at the internal wall of his chest. Trembling, his lips reached her forehead and glanced a whisper of a kiss upon her. He looked at his comrades, the pleading in his eyes almost screamed to them to help her, to bring the woman he loved so much back to him. The women of the household sobbed quietly joining with his agony, their hearts reaching out to him while holding their own grief as best they could close, fearing to release it, for the pain would surely devour them. The forlorn figure before them, usually so restrained, had lost all pretence as he sobbed uncontrollably, social etiquette driven totally from his senses. His shaking hand reached her beautiful, vacant none seeing eyes and drew down the eyelids. The world did not deserve a woman of such beauty to behold it, and this mortal plain had failed her. Spartacus stood away from the crowd and in the distance he watched the figures on horseback gradually become fainter and fainter. His wife approached him and grasped his arm,

'Not now my love, that man is dangerous and enough people have lost those they love this day.'

'You know I will follow him?'

'I would expect nothing else from the man I married, but tonight you are needed close.'

Spartacus approached the body of Bull, young Plinius was still holding his friend,

'By the Gods how did you find your way out here, old friend?' Tictus heard Spartacus' question,

'My father and Epionne came from the fortress to gather flowers. When Bull saw they had left the safety of the walls he went after them, knowing the riders to be close. He made me promise I would not follow, he saved my life, I think he knew it was suicide but he went anyway.'

'Bull was always the bravest of us,' said Plinius.

'He said he gave his word to Cassian and would not break it.'

'I am sorry for the loss of your father Tictus.' In truth Spartacus never really cared for Crannicus but Tictus showed real promise of the man he could become, and so Spartacus wished him only the best.

'My father was a fool Spartacus, but he would not run from Flabinus. He died trying to save Epionne, sword in hand.'

'Then he should be honoured, as all fallen warriors deserve,' replied Spartacus.

'The thing is Spartacus, if he had died running away like a coward, it would not have diminished the love I felt for my father.'

Those that had fallen were loaded on to a cart by their loved ones and the journey back to the fortress began. Cassian did not move and so he stayed on the hill, his wife's body in his arms, alone in his grief. As the sun fell he returned to the fortress. He carried Epionne as gently as a first time mother carries her new born child. The gates opened but no words were spoken. He took Epionne to their bedroom where he laid her upon the bed. He sank to her side and wept. Flora took Cassian's sons, she would not permit them to see their father's grief and besides caring for them took away the horror of her own grief. Tictus hardly left her side, a love which struggled to grow while his father was alive suddenly seemed to prosper in the most dramatic of times. Two days went by and still the door to Cassian's room remained closed, the fallen had been honoured with all the tradition the sorrowful mourners could muster, but Epionne's body remained with Cassian.

Spartacus was never too far from Plinius for he had real concern for the young warrior. Spartacus knew that when Plinius' brother had been slain, it had been Bull who had stepped into the role as brother and protector. The veteran soldier had allied himself

117

with the young Plinius despite the danger doing so placed him in. The centurion and optio who were responsible for the ill treatment of Plinius and his brother could have easily extended their wrath onto Bull. Plinius had survived because of Bull, he had now developed into a fine warrior with few men being able to match his speed or skill. However Spartacus knew the young warrior to have a potentially fatal flaw, and that was his anger. His emotions were never too far from the surface within him, and this could lead him into ill-thought out actions. Spartacus prayed Chia would bring a much needed calm to his spirit, though in truth he held out little hope.

Chapter IX

Spartacus did not have to wait long before the tormented Plinius displayed his anger for all to see. The very next day Spartacus was awoken by shouts from outside his quarters. Before he was properly awake his wife burst into the room,

'Spartacus! Hurry! He is going to kill him.'

Without hesitation the warrior leapt to his feet and raced from the room, not even delaying to gather his weapons. A crowd had gathered, the mob was always keen to see bloodshed. He swatted them aside to get to the spectacle at the centre of the disturbance. Before him stood Plinius, his tunic splattered with blood. At the young warrior's feet was the guard who, so foolishly, allowed Crannicus to leave the fortress.

'On your feet or, so help me, I'll gut you where you lie,' spat Plinius, his rage evident.

'That's enough Plinius. The man has clearly had enough,' called Spartacus, but his words were ignored. Plinius seemed oblivious to all those around him and he slowly pulled his blade from its sheath, at the same time taking a step closer to his prey.

Spartacus moved forward, placing a restraining hand upon the young warrior's shoulder, but his young friend twisted away and without looking, flicked out his blade opening up a cut across Spartacus' torso. There was a sudden intake of breath from all in the crowd, amazed at what they had seen. This could not fail to get Plinius' attention. He looked back to see the what his actions had created,

'Forgive me Spartacus, I never meant to-' Plinius began,

'Apology not accepted, I'm sick of you behaving like a spoiled child.' Spartacus' voice was low and dangerous.

'Spartacus wait!' Aegis tried to intervene, sensing the tension rising between his two friends.

'No Aegis, let's hear what he has to say!' interrupted Plinius, the heat of his temper obviously beginning to rise once more.

'I am not going to say anything,' replied Spartacus, and before Plinius had even realised what was happening Spartacus struck him, sending him sprawling, his blade sent spinning across the courtyard. The blow was powerful and many would not have risen for some time, but Plinius was on his feet in a heartbeat. He came charging, his fist aimed at the jaw of Spartacus, who simply swatted the ill-thought out blow to one side. In the same movement he brought up his knee to catch Plinius in the groin, which caused him to stumble and, eventually, slump to the floor. Plinius tried to regain his feet but, as he did so, Spartacus caught him with a well aimed kick to the side of the ribs. Again the young warrior would not yield. His eyes streamed with tears of anger, and his nostrils flared like a wild beast. Again somehow he made it to his feet and he charged. He threw out his right fist but this time Spartacus simply caught his hand and held it, vice-like, preventing movement. Plinius bellowed out his anger and tried to release himself. He twisted and tried to make contact with his other fist, but again Spartacus caught his hand. For a moment he struggled wildly, Spartacus grasping both of his hands and holding them tight. Chia cried as she watched her loved one, she knew all the love she had tried to bestow on him had not managed to calm him and the torment he suffered. Plinius looked up at the powerful warrior who now prevented his movement. He gazed into Spartacus' eyes and saw only concern, not the hatred he had expected. It was this kindness which felled him far more effectively than any blow which could be delivered. As Spartacus chanced releasing his hands, Plinius' body slumped and then he sobbed,

121

'He's dead Spartacus.'

'I know my friend, but let us not dishonour his sacrifice,' Spartacus replied, his tone now much gentler.

'I am sorry Spartacus, I never meant to harm you.'

'You were forgiven the moment it happened. Come let's tend your wounds.'

The guard watched the two warriors walk away. Deep inside he knew that it was his failures that led to the deaths of those held dear in this household. The beating had been deserved, the shame he felt pulled at his insides and the very next morning he would slip from the fortress, unable to hold a stare with any within the fortress.

Three days after the death of Epionne, Spartacus once again emerged from his own quarters, his swords in place clearly prepared to leave the fortress. His love rushed to him and kissed him deeply,

'How will you know where to find the man?' she asked. Spartacus held up the papers which Druro had left in Cassian's possession,

'These will guide me I'm sure of it.'

He gathered provisions and, while most of the household were still sleeping, he left the fortress. He had thought to ask if any of the others wanted to join him but decided against it. Cassian was in no fit state and Plinius had given his word to Chia that he would never leave her again. Aegis would have been useful but with Cassian lost in his grief Spartacus believed it better, Aegis' wise words were there to help the mournful Cassian. The road was deserted and, for the first time, Spartacus realised he was completely alone. It had been many years since he had acted alone and at first he thought he would enjoy the moment. But as the time went by, and the dusty track stretched out both behind and to his front, he began to miss his comrades, an uncertain future was always easier if shared.

Flora slipped into the darkened room, her eyes struggling to adjust to the lack of light. They finally fixed upon the figure laid out on the bed. The emotion welled up inside her but she fought it, forcing it to a place deep inside, barring it from her mind. Cassian was kneeling at the side of the bed, his hand holding Epionne's. Flora quietly crossed the room and realised Cassian was sleeping. Tear stains tracked down his face and Flora wondered how long he had fought the tiredness, not wanting to let Epionne's beauty escape his vision. Flora touched his exposed forearm, he stirred slightly but did not wake, so she covered him with a cloak. She moved around to the other side of the bed to be closer to her sister, her hand reaching out stroking the cold pale cheek. A tear rolled down her face, but again she angrily forced the emotions away,

'You were always so pretty,' she said, continuing to lightly caress her sister. 'All the flowers at my villa could not rise to your splendour. I used to be so jealous but you were as kind as you were beautiful and so it passed. I just loved to be near you. I'm going to do your hair, you know how you liked it.'

Finally the tears came, the battle was lost and emotions breached the defences and consumed Flora. She was so lost in her grief, Cassian's waking went unnoticed. He came to her side and placed an arm around her shoulders and, for a while, no words were spoken, the two of them lost in their shared grief and loss. Flora eventually regained some of her composure,

'When do you leave?'

'Leave? I'm not leaving, my boys will need me,' replied Cassian, surprised at Flora's words. 'I have already lost a wife and been robbed of holding my child close, I will not lose my sons by chasing a demon.'

'Spartacus has already left, he will need help. Going after a man like that on his own would be unwise.'

'I never asked him to,' replied Cassian.

'No, my dead husband asks you to. Your friend Bull and...' Flora stopped, choking back the tears which threatened to come again, 'and Epionne asks you to. This deed cannot go unpunished Cassian.'

Cassian was surprised at Flora's need for reprisals, but Flora continued despite his shock,

'If I were a man Cassian, I would hunt this man to the gates of Hades if I had to.'

'And what would you do once you found him?'

'I would kill him. I would rip him to pieces, until I had utterly destroyed the man.'

Cassian looked down at Flora. The tone in her voice was matched only by the fervour in her eyes and he knew what she said to be the truth. he would indeed destroy Flabinus for the crimes he had committed against her family. He wondered whether the usually carefree woman who once loved all the world and its beauty would ever return. He glanced back at Epionne and, deep inside, where there had been only sadness a small faint spark ignited the flames of anger. He strode from the room, his voice boomed out orders. Cassian had awoken from his torment and his entire soul now ached for vengeance.

Plinius sat watching Cassian, his heart was heavy for the loss of Bull. He could not imagine life without the eternally joyful old soldier. He wished he could meet Flabinus but he had made a promise to Chia which he would not break, but still he yearned for retribution. He felt a gentle hand brush his cheek,

'Lost in thought my love?' Chia asked.

'I was thinking of Bull, he was a good man.'

'He will always be with you, true friendship never leaves us,' she paused. 'Do you think Cassian will find Flabinus?'

'He will, although what the result of such a meeting will be only the Gods know.'

'This Flabinus is truly a dangerous man,' said Chia thoughtfully.

'Anyone who could better Bull and, by the reports I have heard easily, is a very dangerous man indeed.'

'Can Cassian defeat him?'

'No, I don't think he can. But sometimes the Gods smile upon us.'

'Then he will need his best men with him. Lathyrus, Aegis and Tictus are already preparing to leave. You best hurry.' As she spoke Plinius looked at her, shocked at what she was saying,

'I made a promise to you, I will not break it.'

'You promised not to leave me, that is not the case I'm sending you away.'

'But why?'

'Because I tire of you,' she laughed, 'because from the moment I met you, I knew you were a man of honour. In your heart you will feel you have an obligation to those that have died and those that grieve their loss. I will not be the reason you feel shame.'

'But…' she pressed her fingers against his lips.

'Go kill this man, then come back to me.'

'You are wonderful,' replied Plinius as he kissed her.

'I hope you think so when I am so big your arms won't stretch around my waist.'

For a moment he looked at her, confused by her words, but as the meaning registered within his mind, a broad smile erupted upon his face. He went to whoop with joy but she stopped him,

Now is not the time to show too much happiness my love,'
nodding in the direction of Cassian. 'Hurry back for I would have
you back for when our daughter is born.'

'A daughter, you know this?'

'A woman always knows. Now go!'

Cassian was, as expected, quiet upon the road. Once the
preparations had been completed, and the start of the journey
embarked upon, he seemed to slip once again into his melancholy.
Much more surprising was the mood of Lathyrus. The man was far
from his usual boisterous self. The men around him guessed it was
because of the respect he felt for Cassian, not wanting to upset the
young Roman by being too jovial when so much pain had been
endured. In truth it was guilt that had been eating away at the large
man. Cassian had asked Lathyrus and his men to stay at the fort
and help protect the families. However, Lathyrus had refused,
stating that he had not signed up to care for women and children.
Cassian had relented and the men of the sea had gone to war
against the assassins of Flabinus. The fact that both he and his men
had acquitted themselves well in the battle counted for little, for
Lathyrus now believed it was his short-sighted ego which had cost
the lives of those he had come to care for. From the moment

Cassian had emerged from his room Lathyrus had found it impossible to speak to, or even be in too close proximity, of the man. The guilt tore at his insides and when he glanced at the young Roman his feelings doubled and he quickly looked away, in case Cassian should notice.

The group stopped short of the port, there would be no vessels leaving at this time of day. Cassian decided to make camp and seek transport at first light. Aegis and Plinius gathered wood for the fire while Tictus and Lathyrus busied themselves preparing food. Cassian stood alone, gazing towards the setting sun, images of Epionne floating through his mind. Plinius watched him for a while,

'This task ahead of us Aegis will only bring sadness.'

'You think so Plinius?' replied Aegis, surprised by the sudden change in his friend.

'No person could have cared for a fellow warrior more than I for Bull, but what will tracking Flabinus down achieve? It will not bring my friend back.'

'Oh, in that you are right,' replied Aegis cryptically.

'Speak Aegis! Don't make me guess what you think,' said Plinius.

129

'Flabinus is not like other men. He has become a personal evil to many upon this journey, he must be destroyed. Besides the man is still dangerous.'

'How? The man has no men to speak of, and so these men about us have little to fear.'

'Flabinus could have ridden straight for the port but he went to the fortress. He could have let Epionne live or at least have taken her to use as a bargaining tool. But instead he didn't strike at the fort and he simply killed Epionne to cause as much harm as possible. This is a man who does not consider defeat, if he is not tracked now then he will return. Spartacus understood, that's why he left so quickly.'

'And why did Spartacus leave by himself? He knew we would want to accompany him.'

'Isn't it obvious? Spartacus guessed Cassian would rouse from his grief and give chase and he would require assistance. Plus I believe he has worked out that Flabinus is no ordinary man and if any of us are to cross swords with the man, then it had best be him.'

'Playing the bloody hero again,' Plinius shook his head.

'Ah! haven't you worked it out yet,' replied Aegis, smiling at the young warrior.

'What?'

'He is a bloody hero, though he tries very hard not to be, he can't help it. An internal force drives him on to greatness, bathing us mere mortals in shade.'

'Has anyone ever told you, that you talk complete shit?'

'It has been mentioned,' replied Aegis, a huge broad grin spreading upon his face.

The night wore on, the men hungrily began taking on nourishment. Cassian eventually joined the group for warmth at the fire and, for a moment, silence descended upon them,

'It is important that we as men carry out this task, but we must do it without heavy hearts,' said Cassian

The men looked at him, surprised by his words, for they could not fathom how a man who was devoted to his wife could not have a heavy heart.

'I feel the same anger and guilt as many of you. When I first looked at the body of my wife I was wracked with guilt that I could not prevent her death. But the blame for those we loved dying falls at the feet of one man, Flabinus. From this point let us not torment ourselves as I know some are doing, but look forward to finding the true culprit.'

Lathyrus felt as though Cassian was speaking directly to him but he was not alone, all had similar feelings. However the words from their friend, who had endured so much, lifted their spirits and soothed the demons which snapped and clawed at their souls. The night wore on and although the mood of the camp was far from jovial, it was more like the mood to be expected from men on a mission. Those that felt guilt and held a furnace of pure hatred for the man who had committed the crimes against their family and friends were not able to disband those feelings, however with the words of Cassian they were able to focus more clearly on the task in hand. The group found out from Cassian that Spartacus had left clear instructions of the route he was going to take and therefore it would be possible, with luck, that they may catch up with him.

The fire crackled and, as the group began to slip into slumber, Aegis took the first watch for bandits who roamed this land like another. They could not afford to be caught unaware, and robbed of their chance of revenge. He sang a thoughtful and yet haunting melody which seemed to perfectly sum up the mood of the camp. The men slipped from the real world into dreams and nightmares.

Aegis gazed upon the figure of Cassian, the back of his friend highlighted by the flames that flicked from the fire like wicked serpent tongues. Though Cassian made no sound Aegis was sure that he was still awake. Aegis wondered if Cassian would be able withstand the torments which the Gods had delivered upon him. In such a short time the man had lost his brother, home, unborn child and wife. These were truly a test for any man's soul and still it seemed the Gods would test him further in the task which lay ahead.

Chapter X

The group entered the small port and it wasn't long before a figure hailed Cassian from the shadows. His men drew their weapons but Cassian held up his hand to prevent them taking any rash actions. The man was one of Cassian's operatives, a gentleman of the night who plied his trade in the shadows of this port. He was a trusted agent who had served Cassian's father many years before. They greeted each other as friends, the agent showing great sadness when discussing Cassian's loss. There was a great deal of talking, with the agent becoming animated and pointing towards a small tavern which stood just a stone's throw away from the vessels in the dock. Finally the discussion was at an end, with a shake of the hand and an exchange of coin the agent slipped back into the shadows and was gone.

'We have a problem.' Not waiting for an answer Cassian continued, 'Spartacus missed Flabinus.'

'Has he gone after him?' questioned Tictus.

'That was his plan, but Flabinus had laid a little trap.'

'He's not'

Cassian held up a hand to prevent further questions,

'As far as we know he is still alive but as to his condition that would be merely guess work.'

'So where is he?' The anxiety was etched clearly upon the faces of his men, but it was Plinius who voiced his concern.

'That I do not know.'

'Shit! What are we supposed to do, if we don't know where he is?' Plinius asked, a desperate note entering his tone.

'I said I did not know the whereabouts of Spartacus,' replied Cassian carefully, 'but I know the location of the scum who was paid to delay him.'

'So let's go see this scum, and convince them to enlighten us to where Spartacus is now.' Plinius was ready for action rather than words.

It wasn't far to the small tavern and the group tried their hardest to look like mere weary travellers requiring refreshment. They entered and ordered drinks and proceeded to find suitable seating. Plinius raised the goblet to his lips and was about to take a sip,

'Don't drink that!' Cassian ordered. In a low whisper he added 'how do you think they managed to get the upper hand on Spartacus?'

'Bastards!' Tictus snarled.

'My agent told me that Spartacus still gutted three of the scum before they overpowered him. Now I suggest you mingle. Plinius your with me, we need to have a little chat with the man behind the bar.'

The group waited a while and then slowly began to filter themselves throughout the room, gaining vantage points where they could cover any possible threat. Eventually both Cassian and Plinius stood and made their way towards the un-kept, squat little man who occupied the space beyond the bar. The toad-like man was struggling to keep a smile from his face as he patted the heavy coin purse at his waist. A small fortune had been earned and though it had cost him three of his best men, they could be easily replaced. The order had been to kill, but the man believed the slavers who visited this port would offer yet more coin for such a specimen as the man he had been asked to dispatch. The man's mind snapped back to reality, annoyed his day dreaming had been interrupted. His beady eyes focused on the two individuals approaching him.

'Ah! My good friend. Hopefully you may be able to help; we seem to have lost a fellow traveller.'

'What's that to me?' he spat the words out.

'No need for animosity, I would be willing to pay handsomely for information.' Cassian' words seemed to capture the man's interest,

'How much?' The man smirked, his mind raced to thoughts of coin. The thoughts however were cut short as a powerful arm reached quickly and grasped him by the hair. He threw out his hand, grasping for a blade which he always stowed away behind the bar, but he was too late. He was lifted, unceremoniously, over the counter and smashed into the floor.

'What! What are you doing?'
Plinius began to speak,

'My friend here is a deal maker, he likes to smile and use fanciful words until a deal is done. I, on the other hand, have little patience for such things. So tell me what I want to know and tell me quickly, otherwise I will cut you up into little pieces and feed you to the dogs.'

The terrified man managed a sideways glance to two of his men who had remained seated; shocked at the speed of the attack, but now they started to move. A large fist appeared from nowhere and both collapsed from the power of it,

'Carry on with your business Plinius, these two seem tired and are in need of rest,' Lathyrus smiled as he aimed a well-aimed kick to the groin of one of the men who stirred.

Plinius turned back to his captive. At the same time he drew a dagger and watched as the coloured drained from the man's face.

'Good! I have your attention, now where is our friend?'

The captive could not believe this was happening. His mind searched for a way out of the situation which only delayed his answer. Plinius hit him, partly with his fist, partly with the butt of the dagger and a spray of scarlet erupted from the man's nose.

'I said quickly,'

'He's in a building at the end of the street,' the man screamed, pain and fear loosening his tongue.

'How many men guard him?'

The man delayed too long and again his deliberation was met with violence. A fist drove into to his soft abdomen; he doubled over, a fountain of vomit issuing from his mouth.

138

'You're soft, and out of your depth. You had best answer quickly to save yourself embarrassment and pain.' The words were spoken by Cassian who thought how much Plinius had become like Spartacus. Both had a dislike for the pretence of deal making and preferred the direct approach. It wasn't long before the captive told all he knew, fear had got the better of him and so he told all, the location of Spartacus, how many guards, the best way to enter the building unseen and also which vessel Flabinus had taken and, more importantly, the destination of that vessel.

Tictus and Lathryus watched the others leave, they would stand guard. It was important no alarms were given, although Lathyrus doubted this man had the balls for the fight. Lathyrus reached down and took the purse of coin from the man's belt,

'That's a tidy sum, best I look after it for you. After all it's a dangerous world in which we live.' The captive never answered, merely looked at the floor, he dared not defy these men and he would not risk another beating. Lathyrus looked into the street where the remaining members of his group had headed. He wondered if the brave Spartacus still lived, it seemed impossible that such a man would fall to likes of this scum. Tictus seemed to be thinking the same thing,

'May the Gods protect Spartacus for I think will have need of the man, for Flabinus is no ordinary foe.'

'That is true my friend, but I feel our man is not easy to kill. If our comrades get there quickly enough we may yet see Spartacus once again at our side.'

Secretly both prayed for it to be true, when the clouds of danger gather it is best to have a great shield to protect yourself and Spartacus provided that shield. His strength and skill were formidable but it was the man himself they would miss, the more a trial became treacherous the more the man grew in stature. His whole frame seemed to grow when peril came near and when back at home, with his family; he seemed to shrink to almost fragility. He was truly a man designed for war and carnage in the physical sense, but in the mind and heart only family and friendships dwelled.

The reduced group picked its way up the narrow streets. They could see their desired location but, as they neared, they quickly took a side alley which led them around to the back of the building. Here only a small door was available to those requiring entrance, and no windows looked onto the small alley. They waited for a while, observing the building. A man emerged from the entrance coughing, a deep rasping sound. With his back to them he fiddled with his tunic and began to relieve his bladder against the wall. Cassian nodded and quickly Plinius darted from the shadows, eager to close the gap between himself and the man before he became aware of his danger. Plinius' hand clasped over the man's mouth preventing sound, and the all too familiar feel of a cold blade rested against his throat,

'Don't turn around I have no wish to be covered in piss. Now you have a friend of mine, where is he?' The man gulped, and the action made the surface of his throat press even closer to the blade. He glanced around wondering if he could raise the alarm; however Plinius had obviously guessed his thoughts and applied just a little more pressure to his weapon. Finally the man nodded his compliance and the hand covering his mouth moved away just enough to allow him to speak.

'In there,' he gestured with his head, trying to limit movement and avoid the blade.

'I know that, where?' Plinius was insistent, in no mood for tricks.

'Third doorway.'

'How many guards?' As Plinius spoke he applied pressure to the blade, to ensure the man answered truthfully.

'One with the prisoner, two more in the front of the building.'

'Thank you.' His hand moved back across the man's mouth and his captives eyes expanded with shock as Plinius' blade moved quickly across his throat. Blood gushed onto the wall to join the victim's urine where he had relieved himself. His body slumped to the floor, his final twitching mixing the dust of the pathway with the deep crimson ooze. Plinius looked down at the mess and felt only disgust, then waved his friends forward.

Cassian eased the rickety door ajar. Peering inside the smell of dank, rotting timbers met his nostrils. A small torch only partly illuminated the darkness of hallway; he strained his ears, picking up the undeniable sound of laughter. The group moved inside, struggling to become accustomed to the feeble light. They approached the third doorway cautiously, making sure the enemy were not aware of their presence or more importantly, emerge from an unseen entrance. The door was closed but in poor repair and a number of large cracks made it possible to observe those within.

'You killed my brother; I'm going to make this very painful.' The laughing, surprisingly, came from Spartacus,

'Best be quick, for you will be dead soon.'

'You think you can escape, you're going nowhere.'

'I won't have to, before long my comrades will come and it won't matter if I'm dead or not. You will still be cut to pieces.'

The man didn't reply but, instead, simply threw out another fist which smashed heavily onto Spartacus' jaw. He drew back his hand, the pain had been incredible. Plinius made to rush into the room but Cassian held him back, signalling they must be sure as to the location of the other guards. Aegis moved further up the hallway until he had pinpointed exactly where the enemy were, he signalled to Cassian.

'Plinius make this quick! You get Spartacus, myself and Aegis will take the guards if they try to enter the hallway.' Plinius nodded and turned quickly to the room. Once again peering through the crack in the door Plinius saw the man nursing his hand, clearly Spartacus' enemy had decided not to risk further injury to himself and he walked to the far side of the room, where Plinius could see a cudgel leaning against the wall. Plinius knew all too well how much damage such a weapon could inflict. He had killed the murderer of his own brother with such a weapon. It was clear that he must act now, and he must act quickly. In one fluid action

143

he rose and charged the door with his shoulder. The old rotten timbers dissolved under the pressure of such power. The enemy called out the alarm and raised the cudgel to attack, but he was no match for a trained warrior and Plinius simply knocked him out cold with his fist, after sweeping a poorly judged attack aside. Plinius turned to face Spartacus. His naked beaten and bloodied body was suspended from the ceiling by heavy ropes, which were cruelly cutting into his flesh. The skin of his left arm was torn open and a broken bone protruded from it. He was covered in deep cuts and bruises, it seemed not a place on his body had been free from attack. Spartacus raised his head,

'Took you bloody time didn't you?'
Plinius was relieved to see the bruised face smiling back at him.

'Well we had to enjoy the sights of this lovely port first didn't we?'
The sound of men dying emanated from the hallway and, within a few moments, Plinius and Spartacus were joined by Aegis and Cassian. They carefully lowered the Spartacus' bruised body to the floor, being careful not to cause any more agony than was absolutely necessary. Aegis made a makeshift splint for his broken

left arm and pressed special healing herbs into other wounds which needed attention immediately.

'We need to get him out of this place, the air is putrid,' Aegis said, looking concerned at the damage done to his friend.

As he spoke, the enemy who had been knocked cold began to stir. Plinius looked at his beaten friend and moved towards the man responsible for the injuries. The man's eyes finally opened only to be greeted by the sight of a tip of a sword,

'There is a positive outcome to be gained from this situation,' Plinius whispered. The man didn't reply but simply watched the blade, seemingly mesmerised as the torch light danced strange shapes upon it. 'You get to see your brother again.' The sword thrust smashed all before it, skull and brain matter torn apart, the blade only stopped when it buried deep in the earth beneath its victim.

Cassian watched Plinius and noted how easily the young man killed now. It wasn't that he took pleasure in the act, more that it had become an everyday occurrence. It seemed to hold no more relevance than drinking wine from a goblet or changing a tunic. Cassian struggled with the change and, to be honest, he did not know why. On the journey ahead they would all need to kill and probably kill regularly, but the simplicity of the action unsettled him. Aegis lifted Spartacus onto his shoulder and the group slipped from the building as quietly as they had entered.

Chapter XI

The following day the group were gathered in the tavern, Spartacus was in another room recuperating from his injuries. The owner was running around trying to please the group, he did not want to upset the men who had taken over his business. Maybe if he did enough for them he reasoned he would get to keep both his life and his tavern. Cassian rose and walked down the hallway to where Spartacus rested. He slipped carefully through the door, not wanting to wake his friend if he was sleeping. He looked at his friend seeming so vulnerable, his wounds had been cleaned and his arm placed in a new splint. Spartacus' entire body was covered with bruises and swellings. Cassian knew it was evidence of the man's resilience and strength that he still lived; many would have died from such an onslaught of blows.

'Shouldn't you be on your way?' Spartacus spoke gently; too much movement caused him discomfort.

'We will not leave you behind.' Cassian replied.

'But you need to stay on his trail, he's a slippery bastard.'

'Yes but we need you more.'

'You should have left me. Flabinus must pay for his deeds.'

'I have lost enough; I would not lose a friend if it could possibly be avoided.'

The two exchanged a stare. It was remarkable how both could call each other friend, especially considering the past they shared. But friends they were and Spartacus knew he would never had left Cassian behind and so was not really surprised his friend had returned the compliment.

'I never said when it happened Cassian, I am sorry for your loss. Epionne was a sweet and charming women, her passing will be missed.'

'Thank you Spartacus. She was the best of me, everything that I am proud of in my life she gave me the strength to complete.' An awkward silence came after that, both men found talking it that manner difficult, give them throats to cut any day. Suddenly the silence was broken as shouting came from up the hall,

'Stay here,' Cassian said, drawing his sword. Spartacus had noticed he had taken to wearing a weapon at all times. When they had first met it had been rare to see him armed at all. Cassian left the room leaving Spartacus stranded. This left him feeling useless and he tried to rise from his bed. Pain screamed from every part of his body and bile rose in his throat. He slumped back down and even that action caused his head to thump with agony, he cursed but did not try to rise again. There was more shouting to be heard, and then footsteps. They approached his door and stopped for a moment, what could have only been moments seemed to last an age. His thoughts drifted to memories of his family, their beauty floating the mists of his mind. He stiffened, waiting for an enemy to burst in wielding a blade that would surely seal his fate. He decided that no matter his injuries he would not die easily. The door opened slightly and a figure stepped through and, as it turned, Spartacus braced himself for an attack . As the figure turned to face the bed a huge smile appeared upon his face,

'Lazing around again Spartacus?'

'I thought I'd let the others do some work for a change,' replied Spartacus. He hoped his attempt at concealing his relief had worked. 'So Melachus, how come you are here?'

'Cassian sent me and Postus on a fact finding mission. We have only just heard the grave news, it's a bad state of affairs Spartacus.'

Very bad.   Cassian does well to carry such grief; the weight of it must be almost unbearable.'

'The loss of Bull must be felt be all.'

149

'It is. The man was extraordinary; few are blessed with such courage and spirit. If the others feel as I do, then indeed it is a great loss.'

'Indeed.' There was an awkward silence. Men of action often stumble over such conversation, just as a new born lamb struggles to find its feet.

'You have news for us?' Spartacus moved the conversation on, not wanting to dwell on those matters which caused pain far greater than his injuries.

'Yes, we have found out many things, though their importance will be more evident to Cassian no doubt.'

The days passed and Spartacus grew stronger. Soon he felt he had enough energy to move around without too much discomfort. The bruises had changed colour, from the deep black, to murky blues and then to the unsightly yellows which signified their life coming to an end. The numerous swellings lessened and the broken arm, though not healed, proved more of an irritation than the agony it had previously been. Cassian called the owner of the tavern. Quickly the man obeyed, eager to please, like a whipped dog trying hard to ingratiate itself to its master.

'What to do with you, that is the question?'

The man simply stared back; he feared saying the wrong thing. An ill chosen word could seal his fate, and a number of the men in this room would be more than happy to deliver a blow to do just that.

'The problem is you have carried out a grave injustice against us, your life should be forfeit and your property. Maybe I should let Plinius have his way.'

'No please! I will serve you,' he replied, clearly terrified at the thought of being left to the mercy of the young warrior.

'How can I trust such a man? Your service would need to be exemplary.'

'Please! It will be. You have my word, my life is yours.'

Cassian studied the man. He leaned in close, his eyes burning into the man.

'Very well, but fail me and you will die. The carrion birds will feed well on your body but only after you have endured great torment. Do I make myself clear?'

The man nodded, he knew the words Cassian spoke to be the truth. He would never dare to cross this man or his comrades, each one of them could slit his throat in a heartbeat and would not hesitate in the task. He knew from that moment on he was theirs.

Rain hammered down, the noise of which was only drowned out as thunder bellowed its deafening roar. The shutters were closed but they could not prevent the lightening from illuminating the tavern each time it raced across the heavens. The group huddled next to the fire, the flames of which danced as the winds of the storm outside breached the defences of the tavern. Cassian studied the reports of Melachus and Postus, pausing occasionally to drink some wine. He checked them against Druro's reports. The remainder of the group eagerly awaited his findings, they had become bored of life within the tavern. Finally, after many hours, Cassian sat up straight,

'It seems to me that Flabinus' little empire reaches much further and is much more complex than I first believed.'

'In what way?' Plinius asked.

'We knew he had a great number of agents throughout the empire, these gave him both the knowledge and the capability to complete any task set by his masters,' Cassian paused to allow his words to have an impact, 'but from what I can gather from these reports, we are dealing with a beast far more dangerous that I had originally thought.'

'He has influence beyond the empire?' This time it was Tictus wanting to know more.

'Oh yes, far beyond. He can call in a great number of favours. From these reports I can see he has a great deal of influence in many of the great states around the known world and many of the tribal states too.'

'That's impossible,' Spartacus scoffed.

'I wish it were. From what I can see his group have been responsible for quite a number of assassinations and civil unrest in many areas. As I understand it, if Flabinus carries on unchecked then he will not be serving those who make the decisions, he will be the one making the decisions. A truly distasteful vision if ever there was one.'

'Do you think he's building an army?'

'Oh no Spartacus, he has no need for one. Wars and conquests do not come about by one nation simply having a better or larger army than their neighbours. They begin with an untimely death, the careful whispers in an ear, massaging the ego of a tyrant. In short they are caused by a master of the shadows, who will manipulate both the good and evil in man to achieve an end result. Flabinus has grown powerful but he is not yet untouchable, especially now

Crassus cannot openly support him, though I believe if Crassus knew the extent of the man's reach he may well wish him dead like we do. After all the shadows can only hide so many bastards.'

'So how do we stop him?' Plinius asked.

'We will need to track him, using as much stealth as we can in foreign lands. We will need to avoid the traps he will lay for us and hopefully we can catch him before he gathers enough men around him. Then we will corner him and kill him quickly, without fuss.'

Spartacus rubbed his left arm, wishing it was fully mended,

'So when do we start?'

'In just a few days. I must try to work out the journey he will take, he will need to gather men and coin, he has lost a great deal. But be aware, our path will take us to lands where he has all the advantages, traps will be laid and it is likely men will die. He will have allies to call upon and we shall be alone. In short the odds are in his favour.'

'He will need more than that when I stand in front of him,' Spartacus spoke, his bravado rising.

'Not if I beat you to it,' Lathyrus hailed.

The days passed and the storm raged. All the men knew the mission would be dangerous but they eagerly awaited its beginning. The walls of the tavern had started closing in and tempers were becoming brittle as the constant storm and boredom wore the good spirits away. All but Cassian struggled to hold their anger in control, he seemed completely focussed on the task in hand, continuously searching the reports to any insight into the behaviour of Flabinus. He would, from time to time, seek counsel with one of the other members within the group, but mostly studied alone. Aegis observed the man regularly, watching for tell-tale signs of grief or worse that the need for revenge had gripped his soul, for that could spell disaster for the group; men intent on revenge often acted rashly.

'Your opinion Aegis?' Spartacus had observed the watcher.

'Young Cassian has buried his sadness deep, guarding against it constantly.'

'Good.'

'Is it? We shall see,' replied Aegis.

'We need him with a clear head.'

'I realise that Spartacus, but if you put a rock into the top of a volcano, for a time its anger may be abated. But eventually the ferocity will be released and woe will fall to those nearby.'

'That settles it. When we journey you ride with Cassian, I'll ride with Plinius,' he smirked.

Finally the day came to depart. As the group picked its way down to the docks they had to side-step the devastation caused by the storms which had ravaged the surrounding area. This task was made all the more tricky by the thick, glutinous mud which seemed to be covering the majority of all surfaces. More than once an ill-advised step resulted in a fall and a covering of the foul stuff. When Tictus, the first to fall, rose from the mess he was greeted with whoops of laughter but as many more followed suit the air turned thick with curses. Only Lathyrus completed the journey unadorned with a covering of gloop, the years at sea giving him a speed of foot which did not marry well with the sheer bulk of the man. Eventually though the battle against the mud was won and, despite the casualties namely hygiene and pride, the group navigated their way onto the waiting vessel. It was not long before the prow was splitting the waves, carrying the men to far worse dangers than mud. Each of them watched the disappearing, weather-torn docks as they cleaned, as best they could, the muck from their tunics and equipment. Most wondered what future the Gods had in store for them. All except Cassian; he looked out to sea as if searching for a face, the face of Flabinus. His grip tightened upon the side rail, his knuckles showing white as all blood was driven from them, his jaw tightened and deep within a voice sounded,

'I'm coming Flabinus.'

Chapter XII

The days became steadily warmer and the men enjoyed the sun as it soaked through their skin and massaged the muscles below. The vessel had been moving south, the temperature rising as it did so and although, like at the tavern, movement was restricted the mood of the men was light. The breeze and the sun seemed to soothe the frustration at the lack of mobility. The men began to prepare themselves for the task both physically and mentally which lay before them. Training weapons were taken from storage and each man worked hard at improving his speed and skill. In lighter times the men would swim or indulge in a great quantity of wine, the latter being Lathyrus' favourite pass time. Aegis taught Plinius and Tictus how to use the bow, although it was clear he found it frustrating now he could no longer hold a bow himself. The loss of his hand provided many challenges, which occasionally affected even the wise and thoughtful Aegis. However it showed the true spirit of the man and Plinius and Tictus soon developed their skills, and showed themselves more than capable with the weapon.

Tictus revelled in his new found skill. Spartacus had seen Tictus eyeing Plinius a number of times and felt he knew the reason. Tictus was a number of summers older than Plinius, and yet his friend had succeeded in tasks Tictus had only ever dreamed of. If you added in the fact Crannicus was a loving but overbearing father then Tictus had little opportunity to find his own worth in this world. The young man planted a shaft in the very centre of the target again, he whooped with joy and teased Plinius who playfully threw his bow to the floor and the two of them commenced a jovial wrestle.

Time passed until, eventually, a small island appeared upon the horizon, a fact not lost on the passengers who expressed a wish to feel firm ground beneath their feet once more. Cassian, Lathyrus and the owner of the vessel were deep in conversation for some time, and caused a cheer to resonate through the boat as they, finally, announced a landing would be made. The passengers eagerly eyed the island and then the oncoming beach as it neared and before long men were ashore. Goods were ferried to and from the vessel, the crew taking what was needed to set up camp upon the beach. Parties of men were sent to hunt fresh meat and gather wood for the fires and, despite every indication that the island was deserted, guards were set. Lathyrus stood gazing at a rundown building, its occupiers long since departed, a confused look upon his face,

'What is wrong?' Cassian asked him, seeing the old sailors concern.

'I have visited this place many times, Pyras and his two sons usually occupy this building,' he replied, gesturing with his head as he spoke.

'Maybe they moved to the hills when they saw us approach?'

'No, this place is well known to all as a resting place, especially in times of storm. Pyras would normally make a tidy amount of coin from any who land. It is unusual for him to miss the opportunity.'

'Perhaps they left for an easier life, or maybe disease took them.'

'Maybe.'

The answer clearly lacked conviction and, without another word, Lathyrus moved away scanning the surrounding countryside.

Cassian shrugged knowing he had been dismissed by the old sailor, and so concentrated his efforts on organising the men and creating the camp. Finally their work was finished and many of the men decided to wash away the heat of the day with a cooling swim in the ocean. As they did so Aegis and Spartacus returned to the vessel for a few remaining items. Spartacus had lived with danger for most of his life, to the point when he almost felt it long before it arrived baring its teeth. He was feeling one of those moments, the hairs on his body were standing to attention and a shiver raced down his spine. He scanned the countryside above the camp, searching for would-be attackers but the sparse vegetation offered little cover. He turned his attention to the sea crossing the deck expecting to see sails racing towards him, but the waters were calm and devoid of would-be attackers. Sighing, he thought to himself that finally the trials of his life had begun to wear at his nerves and play tricks upon his senses. He suddenly caught movement in his secondary vision, not on the sea or on land but below him.   Not knowing what to make of it he turned,

'Aegis come here!' he shouted.

'What is it?' replied Aegis, almost expecting to see sails closing in on them judging by the alarm within Spartacus' voice.

'Down there, I saw something. It went under the boat.'

'What?'

'I don't know, I'm no sailor. A shadow, a bloody big shadow.'

For a moment Aegis's face was blank but, suddenly, a fearful look of realisation began to spread upon his face. He turned and ran, full speed, to the other side of the boat calling as he went back to Spartacus,

'Sea demon!'

Plinius and the others felt good. The heat of the sun and the heavy work setting up the camp had filled the muscles with tiredness, but now the cool seawater soothed the aches. He glanced towards the vessel where, for some reason, Aegis and Spartacus were waving their arms aloft and clearly saying something. He strained to hear them but, with noise from his comrades enjoying themselves to the full, it was impossible to understand those on deck. Suddenly an ear-shattering scream split the air and, for a moment, the world stopped. The scream had been like no other he had ever heard. Plinius had heard the final cries of dying men and the screams of the dismembered but somehow this was different. It signified pain yes, but far worse than that. It was a scream that suggested to ones soul that all the fear in the world had been released in that single moment. Suddenly he was jolted back to reality and everywhere around him there was chaos. Men swam frantically, aiming for either the boat or the beach. Many did not know why they fled for their lives, they only knew they needed to put distance between themselves and that terrible scream. It was a primal, animal instinct which drove them on, away from the source of the scream which had split the air. Plinius and Tictus reached the vessel at the same time, scrambling for a foothold, eventually being hoisted aboard by Spartacus and Aegis. They hit the deck hard, coughing and spluttering the salt water from their lungs but, to their credit, they did not linger. They rose immediately, wishing only to help friends from the water. As they reached the rail they realised only one swimmer remained close to the proximity where they had all so recently been enjoying themselves. The man moved slowly through the water with a red blanket of bloodied water growing around him. Though none on board could see his injuries, it was evident they must be severe for a slight cut could not produce that amount of blood. As the man moved so slowly towards them, the beast which stalked the water began to circle him. Spartacus pulled a dagger from his tunic and made to enter the water but Aegis threw his powerful arm around him,

'No! Spartacus in there the beast is the gladiator and we are mere weak and feeble prey.'

The scream erupted again, the creature again striking with power and ferocity, shaking the man as if was a piece of bloodied rag. Spartacus looked away, he had seen so much horror in his life but this was too much and that scream clawed at him, twisted his insides. Plinius stared in disbelief, finally recognising the forlorn figure in the water. Postus was now making no effort to close the gap between himself and the boat, he merely groaned his pain to the world. The beast once again circled its prey, clearly keen to feast upon it again,

'Tictus, Plinius get your bows!' Aegis bellowed.

Within moments the familiar thwack of bowstrings could be heard as the two attempted to strike down the creature, but the water acted as a shield slowing and stopping the shafts before they could do any real damage. Only Tictus manage a decent hit, his arrow shaft could be clearly seen just below the huge triangular fin, but it seemed to not even slow the beast down, and it began its third charge at the desperate figure of Postus.

'No! Aim for the man, let's send our friend upon his way.' The two bowmen looked at Aegis, knowing what he said was the only way they could prevent Postus receiving yet more agony, but it was a terrible thing to do. However they turned and both unleashed their deadly shafts which buried deep within Postus' chest. Within moments his head slumped forward, he would feel agony no longer. The creature struck again, but the savagery was

164

not answered by any screams and the beast and what remained of Postus sank beneath the surface, only the red, spreading blanket marking the slaughter which had taken place. A short time later the huge fin was spotted making its way out to sea. The black arrow shaft still protruding from its flank seemed to cause it little discomfort.

The remainder of the day was spent in virtual silence, even Cassian, who had not witnessed the attack, was so overcome by it he retired early. By far the worst affected was Melachus who had spent more time with Postus, indeed they had become like brothers in the time since the death of Dido. Carrying out missions for Cassian they had come to rely upon each other and now Postus was gone. Melachus left the group and walked into the hills.

'Will he be alright?' Plinius asked Aegis.

'We must hope, for he cannot be angry at a beast. Also Melachus is no soldier, so venting his grief through battle is not open to him. We can only pray the Gods take pity upon him and bring him back to us.'

'The Gods,' Plinius scoffed 'what good do they do any man?'

Aegis smiled. 'That is a question each man must ask himself, and one I cannot answer for you Plinius.'

'I did not mean to offend Aegis, I know you hold the Gods in great esteem.'

'No offense was taken Plinius. Do you not think I have questioned my beliefs? To be honest I continue to do so, for I cannot say I am happy to see good men die and those that deserve to die, prosper.'

'So why believe?'

'For me, it's a young warrior brought back from the very point of death, it's the breeze that makes the leaves sing as it brushes by them, or the moment I held my first born within my arms. I cannot believe that it is all mere chance Plinius but, as I say, you must ask the question of yourself.' As he finished Spartacus approached the young man looked at his friend,

'Spartacus, what say you on the Gods?'
Spartacus thought about the question, as if deciding whether to divulge his inner feelings,

'Truly, I have little to thank them for, but I am alive and I believe it is better to have them on your side than against you, but don't rely on them. Rely on yourself, your true friends and your sword. If that is not enough then you are buggered,' he laughed.

The morning came and the camp burst into activity but the mood was muted. All busied themselves with the task ahead, sparing no time to talk. As the morning wore on Spartacus and Plinius went into the hills to try and find Melachus but without success, and eventually they returned giving up the task, deciding it was clear he did not want to be found. Before setting sail Cassian ordered some provisions and a small craft were to be left upon the beach, he would not leave a good man to starve. The absence of Melachus seemed to force the mood even lower, for they had lost two good men without even drawing a sword. Amongst the sailor population the whispers of a cursed mission began to gather pace, Lathyrus spotting the signs of an unhappy crew and he was all too aware of the dangers of a mutinous crew. He spoke of his concerns to Cassian and Spartacus, the passengers would wear their weapons from that point. The once contented vessel had become a cauldron of tense mistrust, all waiting for that moment which could fan the flames of mutiny across the deck, causing certain death to those too slow to react.

A lone figure trudged its lonely journey of despair, the hills seemed to answer his vulnerability by closing in around him, hiding him from the rest of the world. He finally came to a stop

167

and rested upon a large rock and stared to the heavens. He searched the clouds and, as they moved before his eyes, he suddenly realised he was looking into the face of his old friend Postus. Melachus managed a weak smile, glad to see his friend again,

'I am sorry my friend, if it had been within my power you would never have been taken from us.'

The shape did not answer but continued to smile down serenely, no trace of sadness could be observed upon its features. So at peace the vision helped release Melachus from much of the heavy grief which weighed down his heart.

'What now my friend, what course shall I set?'

As he spoke a strong breeze blew the clouds giving the illusion Postus had turned his head and, as Melachus followed the path of that gaze, he saw that its path led to the one gap in the hills. There, down in the cove, sat the small craft Cassian had made available to him,

'It seems my travelling days are not over, but know this my friend you will never be far from my thoughts, and the name of Postus will always be honoured by me.'

The breeze rose again and the features of Postus drifted away.

Melachus sat for a while until the very last of his friend had

disappeared, he stood and began his journey.

Chapter XIII

The rain swept down forcing both passenger and sailor to pull their robes up closer to their exposed necks. It had been two days since the loss of Postus, a loss which had stretched the moral of the crew to breaking point. When the journey had begun, the vessel had been a place of relative excitement and optimism. Both sailor and passenger freely moved amongst one another, but now when the work was done, small groups formed and the whispering started. Startled glances over the shoulder betrayed their guilt, as the passengers became aware that the men they sailed with, who only a few days earlier they called friend, could no longer be trusted. The weather seemed to echo the boats feelings, as heavy rain and strong winds hammered the deck and those upon it. Lathyrus signalled the passengers they grouped towards one end of the vessel,

'It will not be long now,' whispered Lathyrus.

'So they mean to mutiny, but on a night like this,' replied Cassian.

'Tell me Cassian, when would you rather fight a bunch of land lovers, when the decks are calm or when the waves are striking?'

'I see your point, so what to do? We are clearly outnumbered.'

'Tell me Lathyrus, with the men here could we sail this vessel?' Spartacus asked.

'If the weather calms, we would stand a chance but if the Gods blow us misfortune then we would probably be taken to the bottom.'

'And if our rebellious friends get there way?'

'Throats cut and overboard.'

'Then I suggest we take this boat, and those who will not yield take a swim.'

They nodded their agreement, drawing their weapons as they turned to go in search of the sailors who would cast them into a watery oblivion. As it was the search was short lived, as around thirty sailors approached from the other side of the ship. They too brandished weapons and were intent on causing bloody mischief upon their passengers. Spartacus counted the numbers they now faced, and realised a number of the crew were missing. He scanned the surrounding area and soon spotted a number of sailors who had been made to sit on the deck and had been relieved of their weapons. Cassian spoke first,

'We do not have to do this, we will be reaching land in a few days and you will never see us again.'

'With you on board we will probably never see land, the Gods have forsaken you.'

'Bollocks!' Spartacus roared, 'I guarantee that if carry on with action, you will all be dead before sunrise.'

His words brought the owner of the vessel to the front, who took care to stay well back in case Spartacus charged,

'You are out matched, throw down your weapons and you will not be armed.'

His words were met with laughter by Lathyrus,

'Both you and I know that is not how it works, let me say this, if you persist in this course of action, by the end of it, even your own mother wouldn't recognise your body. Now from one old sailor to another, throw down your weapons.'

A frightening stillness settled between the two groups, each group recognised that one move could very well set of a ferocious skirmish, an encounter which would without doubt leave many of those standing there, dead or dying. The cost of losing such a skirmish would be grave indeed, as out there on the waves there was no code of conduct or the dignified way of treating the

172

defeated. It rarely happened on land, but at least a healthy man would be sold into slavery rather than slaughtered. However the victorious would not want an enemy so close on a vessel which restricted movement, and so both sides knew this was victory or death. Plinius looked at the men who stood ready to cut his throat, he knew they were not warriors but sailors were tough men, they had to be, for a life at sea tested a man to his limit. The sea could be cruel and deceitful, one moment pleasant and calm and then in the beat of a heart, a raging beast which tried to snatch them from the pitiful haven of the vessel. Plinius' eyes came to rest on one such sailor, his skin baked like the hide of a cow, tough and unyielding. A scar ran from the top of the man's brow to the base of his chin, his shoulders as broad as an ox. Not a man you would normally trouble yourself to pick a fight with. Plinius stared at the man, and then the man was staring back, both willed the other to yield. Plinius smiled and blew the man a kiss and the world dissolved into carnage, his opponent enraged by the young whelp who taunted him. The passengers had prepared well, shields and blades rising in unison, the endless training in deadly combat more than a match for the sailors. Their opponents were tough men, hardened over the years by what the sea threw at them, but this was

173

not some fist fight in a tavern. The superior numbers quickly dwindled, their advantage slipping, the sailors began to retreat. A couple chose to leap into the ferocious water which surrounded the vessel, rather than feel a blade rip the life from them. Most though fought and died as they backed slowly away from the ever advancing gladiators, footing became treacherous as blood mixed with the salty water which crashed upon the deck. Cassian lost his footing and went down, seeing an opportunity for a quick kill, two sailors moved forward but as they did Cassian's men closed around him using their shields to protect their friend. The two sailors now more advanced than their comrades were isolated, and soon fell to a number of slashes and thrusts. The screams of the dying men would have been deafening, but even that noise was drowned out by the cascading waves which stormed all about. Time and time again sailors crashed to the deck, no quarter given as the killing blows rained in to ensure they would never rise again. Spartacus received a slight cut to the shoulder, however in did not even slow his own stroke which took the head from his enemy.

Before long the last of the mutinous crew had been dispatched with only minor injuries to the gladiators who had dealt with the difficulties the sea had thrown at them with contempt. They turned in unison and approached those sailors who had been relieved of their weapons by the former and now dead owner of the vessel.

'Why did you not fight for your master?'

All but one of the sailors looked away, fearing to hold the gaze of the wealthy Roman who had just proved himself to be more than a mere spoilt politician.

'Their actions were a betrayal of this vessel and the men aboard, we tried to convince them to merely put you ashore, but they would have none of it.'

'Well they have paid for their actions, now will you join us?' The men glanced around at each other, though there was little choice in accepting Cassian' offer, and to a man they nodded their agreement. Cassian spied each of the men in turn, trying to gauge the quality of each, many avoided eye contact fearing the Roman aristocrat would change his mind and send them to the depths. All but the man who had spoken previously, faltered under his stare and so Cassian engaged this man, who he judged to be a natural leader.

'What's your name?' he asked the man.

'Dion, my lord.'

'No need for such titles, my name is Cassian. We eat, sleep and fight together and if need be we die together is that clear?' His eyes scanned all before him now. 'Dion this vessel is now yours, the men around you are the beginning of your crew, you will work for me and be paid well for it, are there any questions.'

'No Cassian, we will serve you well.'

'That goes without saying,' Cassian turned a strode to his friends eager to check all were well and suffering no serious injury.

'Can they be trusted?' Spartacus asked.

'Only the Gods know, but Lathyrus if you would be so kind as to keep them very busy, tired minds and bodies find it hard to plot.'

'So what now Cassian?' Plinius enquired.

'We have a few days before we reach our destination, it may take longer with this crew and we will all have to lend a hand, especially if the weather worsens.'

The group looked to the heavens and then realised that as the small battle had met its end on the decks then so too, had the storm blown itself out. The waters lay calm and the wind just stroked the cheeks as a gentle breeze. As the sailors who had fallen in battle were tipped from the vessel to be welcomed by the waves, tiredness seemed to overtake the remaining passengers. The fight had been short but hard, it sapped at the muscles. Coupled with the suspicious nights on the vessel before hand, where few slept, preferring to keep an eye on the mutinous crew. So as the weather calmed so did the men, they slipped to slumber with just a few men to watch over them, even Cassian closed his eyes though all doubted his mind would be filled with dreams of delight and happiness. Those that were still awake observed the man and his unsettled slumber, his cries for a loved one lost, his pleading for forgiveness. The shame of failing clearly ripping at his heart, Spartacus approached his friend and for a moment was still just observing the torment that he was powerless to stop. He lifted a cloak and placed it gently upon his friend and hoped the extra warmth would drive the cold and fear from him. In time his moans settled and were replaced with a tired man's snores, accompanied by many others as the hours passed upon the salt and blood ridden decks.

......As the rising sun warmed the bodies and its unwelcome rays forced open the eyes of tired men. Cassian was already up gazing over the side deep in contemplation. For a time his friends left him be, but as the day passed they included him in the trivial conversations, that often happen as men try to avoid those types of discussions that tear at the insides. The avoidance worked and before long Cassian seemed his old self, plotting the way ahead for his men, checking on the condition of the vessel and men at regular intervals. Dion seemed to attach himself willingly to Lathyrus keen to learn all he could from the old sea dog, something that Lathyrus seemed to enjoy immensely. He hadn't had much opportunity lately to bestow the tales of Lathyrus, his wondrous adventures and deeds, the beasts he had destroyed and the ladies he had bedded. A young man eager for each tale was too much for Lathyrus to ignore, and the old swagger came back to him as he recounted his Herculean achievements.

'By the Gods, there goes the peace and quiet,' Spartacus said, though smiling as he did.

'He has achieved much in his life,' Aegis added.

'He's a lying old rogue,' Cassian spoke but then added more kindly 'but our rogue.'

'That he is, but sometimes it would be nice if he was someone else's.' The group burst into laughter, they watched Lathyrus as his gestures became ever more flamboyant and the tales more and more incredible, but even more amazing was the look on Dion face, like a man dying of thirst he drank in the tales ever eager for more. Spartacus too was listening and finally was beginning to understand the old rogue, with each tale was an education he had not seen it at first but now it became clear that Lathyrus was instilling an education, and the recipient did not even know. Each tale placed sailors in danger, each tale told of how when the correct methods were used, then those sailors sailed into the sunset, and those that took the wrong option sank to the depths and a watery grave.

'The clever old bastard,' Spartacus whispered to himself.

'A most impressive way to pass on knowledge,' added Aegis upon overhearing Spartacus' comment. The vessel moved with ease and it seemed to all that since Lathyrus had been giving instruction the waters lay still and calm and just enough wind blew to fill the sails and speed them upon their way. His masterly display made a mockery of the previous captain's attempt at sailing. Spartacus had believed the former owner to have been competent, but now seeing Lathyrus go to work showed him just how wrong he was. The vessel now seemed to dance above the waves, and answered the will of Lathyrus as though it were some mystical extension of his own body. Even the sailors performed their duties with far more urgency and efficiency, often in place even before Lathyrus shouted an order. Spartacus watched how the large man moved, for such a big man he was nimble and moved in perfect rhythm with the vessel. He supposed that this was the reason why Lathyrus was such a fine hand to hand fighter, for he used the same rhythm, and coupled with the agility, made him a formidable man to face.

Chapter XIV

Land was sighted on the third day after the mutiny was put an end to, a collective sigh of relief could be heard from the passengers. The journey had been long and perilous and each doubted the next stage of the journey would be any safer, but at least it would be on firm ground where all felt far more at home. It had taken some time to negotiate the vessel into a place where the passengers and their cargo could disembark, the sun dropped from the sky and an enclosing darkness was upon them before they had finished making camp. Cassian sat near the camp fire head buried in papers,

'May I ask a question?' Plinius asked nervously, sometimes the difference in social standing still made him uneasy.

'Of course,' replied Cassian not moving his eyes from his plans.

'Where are we and what is it we must do?'
Cassian raised his head and stared intently and the young warrior, for a moment he looked as though in deep contemplation,

'You are right Plinius, fetch the others it is time for all to know more.'

It took time to gather all the men, some were gathering firewood, others like Spartacus checking the surrounding countryside ensuring the camp would be safe from attack. Eventually they all came to be seated around the growing flames, Cassian sent Dion and his men to prepare the vessel, for they would be setting sail at first light. Cassian waited for quiet and then began,

'We have left Greek shores behind us, just a day's ride over those hills will bring us to the city of Cyrene.'

'Why not sail directly into its port,' Spartacus asked,

'Because we are more concerned with its surrounding countryside, this place has been the location of great political unrest and Flabinus has been right at the centre of it,' Cassian paused as if choosing his words carefully, 'these lands have only recently become a Roman province.'

......'I bet that has made the inhabitants happy,' suggested Spartacus sarcastically.

'It's more complicated than that, these lands were not conquered but left to Rome by the former ruler. To the majority of the populace it makes hardly any difference who is making the rules, in fact for many it has only made them more prosperous.'

'So where does Flabinus come in?' Plinius asked.

'Cyrene in the past opened its arms to people from all over the known world. All were treated fairly and had equal rights, but that has changed. One such group, who originate from Judea have found that the freedom to act as any other citizen, has been eradicated.'

'Let me guess Flabinus.'

'A prominent land owner who used to speak out against this minority was found butchered along with his family, of course blame fell on those from Judea.'

'So Flabinus is working for Crassus, and Crassus wants to see these people enslaved, or killed what?' asked Spartacus.

'I don't believe so, this is Flabinus' work. I have told you before that Flabinus is out growing the cage in which Crassus kept him, this is his own little project.'

'But what has he to gain?'

'It's my belief that Flabinus is working for those from Judea.'

'But his actions have put there people in danger!' Spartacus said exasperated.

'They are unaware of his guilt, he will be whispering in the ears of those people. Telling lies which they are eager to believe, he will build a fire within them until they are ready to strike and these lands will burn.'

'So what does he gain from this?' asked Plinius.

'These people are not warriors, he will promise them mercenaries and weapons. Anything that their newly fanned hatred desires, they will hand over coin by the wagon load and he will disappear over the sunset, along with their dreams of equality.'

'Surely they wouldn't, not without guarantee's.'

'Flabinus does not simply turn up one day, say give me all your money and then off he goes. He gains trust, sorts out problems, makes troublesome officials go away. He will be the toast of the community, but he will take what he can from them. Money, land, even their lives, and for no better a reason than because he can, because he believes he is strong and they are weak.'

'Well he is strong, and a bastard. But he knows what he's doing,' Plinius stated.

'Does he?' Cassian eyes narrowed 'all the strong men in this world who kill, steal and become a blight on mankind, how many young Plinius sleep soundly at night and do not fear the steps beyond their door?' The words came from Cassian more sternly than he intended.

'I did not mean he was right, I only….,' Plinius words faltered.

'Calm yourself Plinius, I took no offense but you should know that all of us here have carried out duties which we considered to be the right course of action, but the guilt of those actions still grasp at us while we sleep. Flabinus has no just cause or excuse of any type, sooner or later the spectres of his past will catch up with him, whether they be of the mind or those made of flesh.'

'But surely if what you do is true and right why would it weigh down your dreams?'Tictus added, baffled by Cassian' response.

'When you kill a man Tictus, you often look into his eyes. It is then that you see the man, the army or master he serves are no more. Just the man stands before you, the man who takes employment where he can to stop his family from starving. '

' That day will not be the only time his face visits you,' it was Spartacus who uttered the last words, words which lay heavy in the atmosphere.

'So you would rather not kill Flabinus?'

'Oh him, I would kill a thousand times, bastards like Flabinus never return. I think the other world is too keen to keep his treacherous soul.'

'So if Flabinus is so popular in these lands what's stopping his supporters from simply slitting our throats?'

'Truthfully, absolutely nothing,' Cassian replied. 'but my father dealt with the very people that Flabinus plies his trade with now. Hopefully that will at least give me the opportunity to be heard by those that matter.' Cassian continued for some time, going through the details of where they must go and who they must try and see. It seemed a huge gamble to his friends, but they knew Cassian to be a man who studied every detail and would not risk their lives unless the task ahead was achievable. That night the band of men slept uneasily, anxious at what the next day would bring, some dreamt of those loved ones left behind, others of the loved ones who were lost to them forever. Aegis' slumbering thoughts were different, he remembered back to the camp of

Flabinus before it was over run and most of the assassins killed. He remembered a figure standing next to Flabinus, a familiar figure though he could only see his back. The man whoever it was, laughed with Flabinus and try as he may Aegis was unable to put either face or name to him. The shape he recognised and he searched his memories for the man, but no matter which dark road within his mind he traversed, the journey was fruitless.

The morning came, the early sun driving away any moisture left by the previous day's rainfall. Most of the men were in fine form, waking and finding themselves on solid ground had been enough to cheer each of them. All but Aegis began the morning with a smile, keeping himself to himself he still agonised over the mysterious figure in his dreams, again and again he recalled the shape of the man, but all to no avail. With each failed attempt came frustration and much deeper than that a terrible feeling of foreboding began to build within the pit of his stomach. The morning wore on as the band trudged through the unfamiliar terrain, the barren golden ground in stark contrast to the greenery of Cassian's lands. Tictus had begun to remove some of his armour struggling against the oppressive heat, only to to receive chastisement from Spartacus,

'We are in foreign lands, where danger could be only a moment away. Now put your bloody armour back on.' Spartacus' voiced had boomed out, reminding Tictus of the battle hardened centurion he had witnessed on a visit to Rome, he flushed with embarrassment. Shocked he fumbled with his armour trying too quickly to reattach it, it was made worse when Plinius strolled by laughing at his friends discomfort. Plinius was rewarded with a torrent of abuse from Tictus, he skipped out of arms way, easily avoiding a playful punch from Tictus. Plinius could understand the urge to remove armour it was already unbearably hot, and it was only just midday. It was made all the worse by the fact that they seemed to be continuously travelling up hill, his armour already feeling as twice as heavy as when he had first put it on. He felt the sweat racing down his back, and wondered if it was worth falling foul of Spartacus just to remove the uncomfortable armour for a few glorious seconds. His thoughts of rebellion were interrupted by Aegis signalling that they were no longer alone, riding parallel to the small convoy were riders, clearly tracking their movements. As the hours passed it was apparent that the riders now on each side were closing the distance between themselves and the convoy.

'Do you think they are closing for the attack?' Tictus asked, his tone betrayed his concern.

'Unlikely, if they wanted to attack they would have left it to the last moment before revealing themselves,' replied Spartacus.

'What then?' this time Plinius asked the question.

'I expect they are herding us towards them,' Spartacus nodded to his front as he spoke.

'Bollocks!' replied Plinius his hand moving towards his sword.

'Hold that action,' Spartacus whispered, 'be ready but keep your hand away from your weapons, let's not start anything prematurely.

The small convoy moved towards the blockade which spanned the dusty track, as it did so the riders on each side gradually reduced the gap between themselves and Cassian's men.

'Aegis a report please,' Cassian asked.

'To our front it looks like at least thirty men, the riders on each side have about eight a piece but they have no bows, and I don't think they have slings. So if they want to attack they will need to get close and to be honest they look more like farmers than soldiers.'

189

'Then we have an advantage,' Cassian replied. His words caused more than a few raised eyebrows within his group, most of them not sharing his confidence. The band moved ever forward, now was not the time to show weakness. When eventually they did stop it was just outside the range of a well aimed spear. A figure walked from the blockade, confidence exuding from his manner, he strolled like a man who knew he had the advantage.

'My name is Orin and I demand to know why you are on our lands?'

'Forgive me if I am wrong but I believe this is a Roman province, and this track is part of no private estate,' Cassian replied.

'We recognise no Roman law here.' Spittle issuing from Orin's mouth, it was clear he had no love for Rome or its people.

'I wish to speak to Dara, be so kind to take me to him.'

'Why should I care who you wish to speak to, maybe I should just have my men gut you here and now.'

'For two reasons Orin son of Dara,' the words shocked Orin how did this Roman know who he was. 'Your father and elder brother would not wish that any member of my family be harmed, for he owes a debt to my father, and therefore to me. The

190

second is you have numbers on your side that is true but I am the only one here who commands warriors and if you attack most of your men will die long before we lay in the dust.' Cassian stared into the eyes of Orin, his look did not falter. Orin however felt the pressure of a leader who had been outflanked and the loss of face in front of his men. He was tempted just to order the attack, but knew if his father heard of it he would be displeased,

'Very well Roman but no tricks or you and your warriors will die.'

Little did Cassian know but at the same time he was encountering the first group of Judeans, the man he truly sought was preparing to leave the same coastline. The preparations were being made for Flabinus to depart from the port of Cyrene. The man stood on the deck of his vessel, he watched the progress and couldn't help smiling to himself. He had concluded his work quickly not knowing if a Roman official would attempt to delay him. He knew from his spies in this port that he had now been made an enemy of Rome, and therefore it would not do to dawdle in a Roman province. He vowed to himself, there would be a day of reckoning with Crassus. In Crassus' service he had carried out many tasks, all of which had increased the Roman senator's wealth and influence greatly. In return Crassus had turned his back when that fool Pompey had crowed loudly in the senate. Flabinus stared down at the dock as the wagons on the port were being unloaded to be placed within the vessel, the Judeans had been most helpful. That had unwittingly provided him with the means to realise his ambition far away from the prying eyes of Rome. He thought of Cassian, a man who had slowed his own progress, he would take revenge on that Roman whelp at the earliest opportunity. He wondered if Cassian had tried to follow his path, or as he suspected slunk into a corner and cried at his misfortune at losing his wife. Not that it mattered to Flabinus, he was prepared for every eventuality, making sure traps were laid along his path. If the Roman did indeed show more backbone than he gave him credit for, then he would be most fortunate to survive any attempt at revenge.

Chapter XV

Many miles away and across the great expanse of water, Spartacus' wife Cynna stared into the countryside from the old fort's battlements. She watched a figure as it moved from place to place but always with its eyes fixed on the long dusty track which led from the fort. Each morning the solitary figure would slip from the safety of the fort, walk quite some distance and gaze hopefully at the road which meandered off towards the horizon. The pregnant Chia had taken to this ritual since her beloved Plinius, had left with Cassian and the others. It had been nearly two months since he had departed, and she was aware her child was growing quickly within her, she yearned for his presence. Each of her days followed the same pattern, optimism, followed by despair and then tears. However, before she returned to the fortress, she would wipe the tears from her face, not wanting the others to see her weakness. She would replace them with a smile and pretend all was well, and they would pretend to believe her. Cynna made sure Chia was making her way back before glancing into the courtyard. She spied another solitary figure tending a small garden, it was Flora, she had planted wild flowers the same type Crannicus and Epionne had gone to fetch the day they died. This was her monument to them, only she tended the minuscule patch of colour in an otherwise drab military building, but somehow the colour of the small garden only added to the sadness of the place. Cynna suddenly felt her own pain and longing for the man she loved, she wanted his arms about her and to see his child-like face as he smiled and made a fool of himself. This was not a happy place, it pulled the soul to despair, she so wished Spartacus would return. They could leave this place far behind, she wondered if he was safe and how many miles lay between them.

Spartacus eyed the armed guards around him, one such guard had tried to hurry him along. However, as the guard had reached out an arm to push Spartacus forward, he recoiled at the warrior's words,

'I am no prisoner boy, I go where I like and at whatever speed I choose, and if that hand makes contact you will draw back a stump.'

The guard had quickly withdrawn his hand and for a brief moment held the stare of the heavily scarred warrior.

'A wise choice, now piss off.'

'Spartacus, play nicely with our hosts.' Cassian spoke in mock chastisement.

The moment did not go unnoticed by Orin, who clearly was regretting his decision not to slaughter the arrogant Roman, he settled for shooting a loathsome look at the man. Cassian merely returned it with his most sickly sweet broad grins, which did nothing for the anger pumping through Orin's veins. He forced himself to walk away, allowing himself to become concerned with trivial things anything to stop him thinking about Cassian. Hills were beginning to appear, in the distance, and as the convoy neared, Cassian was surprised to see how they jutted from the surrounding countryside. There was no gradual climb, they seemed to have simply been dropped there by some careless God. Coming closer Cassian could see the inclines of the hills were strewn with boulders, and here and there caves, and crevices could clearly be made out,

'You could hide an army up there,' Spartacus whispered in Cassian's ear.

'I doubt they have an army just yet, and an army without weapons is just a mob.'

'Still capable of wiping this little band out.'

195

'I am afraid I cannot dispute that point Spartacus, but as a fine gladiator once told me sometimes you just have to stick out your chest and enter the arena.'

'Sounds like a complete fool.'

'Yes you are probably right,' laughed Cassian.

The march into the hills was hard going, the sheer inclines were treacherous and unforgiving. The sun still bore down upon them, sapping ever more energy. Cassian's men, however, would not let it show, this was not a time to show even the slightest weakness. Even Tictus, raw in the ways of a warrior, refused to allow Orin's men to see any sign of vulnerability. Spartacus had observed this and could not help being impressed by the young man, indeed Tictus had handled himself well on this mission, better than he had hoped seeing as the boy came from the loins of Crannicus. They crested yet another hill, but as they succeeded in traversing its summit, they were greeted with an amazing site. The hill was shaped like some giant bowl, a slope from each side ran down to a plateaux. Upon the plateaux, a small village had begun to develop, it was an extremely clever place to set up a base, the village was completely hidden from the surrounding countryside. Not only, that, any approach could be spotted long before it became a danger by just a few well-placed well placed sentries. This would allow the villagers plenty of time to slip away, before any would-be attacker could get close.

The track down to the village was steep but brought a pleasant change than carrying their heavy armour up hill, Spartacus was studying those men around him and also which of the villagers who were now leaving their homes to see the spectacle. He assessed which of them posed a possible threat to himself and his men. Most were simple folk; some carried make do weapons while others just carried a look of curiosity, keen to learn who their new guests were. Then emerging from a crowd a number of elder men, the man leading them wore no armour but merely a simple tunic but his authority issued from every sinew. The crowd became boisterous but quickly calmed at the mere holding up a hand from the man.

'Orin what have we here?'

'This Roman says he knows you,' again the bile evident in Orin's words.

The man walked closer not bothering to call guards to his side, he approached Cassian and for a while just stood and stared at him, time seemed to slow as the man weighed up the young man before him.

'I see the young Cassian has added muscle to his intelligence.'

'In these times it is prudent to have more than one skill, Dara.'

'There was a time when your family called mine friend, and would embrace each other as such.'

'Forgive me Dara,' Cassian closed on Dara and both parties threw their arms about each other. 'For my part our friendship is as true as ever.' Dara could not help that noticing Cassian glanced in the direction of Orin as he spoke.
He broke into laughter,

'Do not worry about Orin, he can be a little too forthright in his opinions of all that is Roman,' as he spoke he gestured that Orin should come closer, 'Orin this man is the son of a dear friend, and therefore, is a friend of our family, you will treat him as so.'

'Yes father,' replied Orin through gritted teeth.

'My people these men may well be Roman, but they are friends, and they are men of honour,' he then turned to Cassian.

'Your family they do well, I was sorry to hear of the death of your father, but Epionne and the boys they do well.'

'May we go somewhere less public we need to talk,' replied Cassian struggling to hide the sadness at hearing his wife's name. Dara nodded his agreement concerned by the cloud that now covered the usually cheerful expression of the young man.

The hut was simple but well cared for, it was the largest of the buildings in the village and so Cassian guessed it was the place where the elders would meet and discuss the issues of the day. Cassian was joined by Spartacus and rather surprisingly Orin had accompanied Dara, the four were seated with wine and food close by. The rest of the men ate outside never too far away from their weapons. Just because a host seemed friendly didn't mean he was and there were a number within the village who seemed to hold the same opinion as Orin.

'So Cassian I take it this is not merely an old friend visiting another.'

'I wish that it were Dara, my visit concerns a man named Flabinus.'

'We don't know any such man.' Orin threw the words out quickly.

'I believe Flabinus has promised you weapons and men, to help in your rebellion and to be honest your response Orin has confirmed my beliefs.' Orin did not answer, just stared back in anger.

'Why does this man concern you?' Dara asked, but within he worried that the villagers had already given so much to the man that Cassian sought.

'He is wanted through-out Rome, the man is a liar, thief and murderer and will be brought to task for his crimes.'

'Why should it bother us how many Romans this man has killed or swindled?' Orin added.

'Because his crimes are not just against Romans, and I believe he may already committed offenses against your people, though you are not aware of them yet.'

'Such as?' asked Dara.

'Most of your troubles started when a prominent figure within Cyrene was murdered, that's when your people began to be victimised. That assassination was carried out by Flabinus, he promised you weapons and men, and I would guess you have recently handed over more coin than you can afford, you will never see that coin again.'

'How do you know this?' Asked Dara the shock evident upon his face.

'Flabinus is a master at deceit, he takes from all he meets and delights in murder and torture. You are not the first to fall to his skills and unlikely to be the last.'

'And why should we trust you Roman and the masters you serve?' Orin again spat out his venomous question.

'I do not care one jot whether you believe me or not, but I will give you three reasons anyway. The first my father's relationship with yours was one he held dear, I would help your family if I could. The second reason for you to trust me is I have contacted Critillo the governor of Utica, he will send enough gold to replace what you have lost and speak to those in power at Cyrene, he will attempt to apply pressure to restore stability to this area. The third reason is personal, I am here not at the whim of some Roman master, Flabinus murdered my wife, and a number of good friends. Whether you believe me or not, it will be inadvisable to align yourself with Flabinus.

'Cassian my dear friend, I am so sorry for your loss.'

'Father you can't just take this man's word,' cried Orin exasperated.

'Shut your mouth, Cassian is a man of honour. Can you not see, or are you so blinded by hatred for all that is Roman, that you are unable to tell the truth with your own eyes and ears?' Dara's words were loud and his voice quivered with anger, Orin shrank away from him. Fearful at the sight he had not seen his father raise his voice in anger for many years. 'From this point Flabinus is an enemy of our people we will take all assistance that is offered by Cassian, and in return we will offer any help that he requires from us, do I make myself clear?'

'Yes father.......it will be done.'

Orin seethed inside, his mind raced asking a thousand questions. How could his father take the word of a Roman, when it was people of Cassian's kind that had mistreated the people of this land? To put such a man above that of Flabinus, who had shown himself to be a true friend of the Judeans, he had witnessed Flabinus time, and time again carry out acts, which proved he was a man of honour. He decided he would not go against the wishes of his father, but neither would he help this Roman entrap Flabinus. Dara began to pour the wine but when he reached the goblet belonging to that of Orin, the young man covered it with his hand.

'Forgive me father, I still have many duties to perform this night,' with that he stood and left, affording Cassian and Spartacus the very briefest of nods.

Dara watched his son leave,

'Alas my friends, I fear my son is reluctant to recognise you with the honour in which you deserve.'

'A man is free to choose those that he calls friend, but be warned Dara, friends of Flabinus tend to end their day face down in the dirt. Flabinus cares not, how many die in his name, indeed he as more regard for the dirt beneath the dead. It would be wise to try and show Flabinus in his true light before Orin is lost to you forever.'

'Youth, if only I was young again Cassian and had the luxury of being so passionate in such matters. I would hunt this man myself, and then there would be a reckoning.'

Chapter XVI

The morning brought about the smoke of freshly lit fires, which drifted upon the light breeze filling the makeshift huts of the village. Spartacus spat the acrid taste of them from his mouth, looking around most of the men were still fast asleep. Plinius however was missing, and it looked to Spartacus as though he had been gone for some time, the old warrior began to worry. Plinius had a quick temper and the village wasn't exactly filled with friends, he jumped to his feet determined to find the young warrior. He emerged from the hut, glancing nervously in each direction, but the only person visible was Orin, who was at that moment wiping blood from his blade.

'Orin where is Plinius?' Spartacus could not help looking at the deep scarlet liquid dripping from the weapon of the man before him.

'Who is Plinius?' replied Orin impatiently. However, then he noticed the anxiety in Spartacus' eyes, 'what's wrong Spartacus worried I may have gutted your little friend. His smile soon disappeared as a powerful hand gripped him by the throat.

'Let me tell you this boy, if Plinius is harmed in anyway way, I will personally remove your balls and feed them to you.'

'Spartacus! Release him, what's going on?' Cassian cried frantically, not wanting tensions to rise further within the village.

'This idiot believes i have murdered one of your men by the name of Plinius,' Orin croaked rubbing his throat.

'Less insults Orin, or by the Gods I will....'

'Look let's just find Plinius,' Cassian interrupted keen to avoid any more trouble.

'One of your men left the camp east, I do not know his name but he looked troubled.' the voice came from Dara. He had emerged from his hut to investigate the commotion.

'Thank you Dara,' Cassian replied.

'I did not hurt your friend Spartacus, but there will come a time when we will discuss what has happened here further.'
The world went black for Orin, the speed in which Spartacus threw the fist was far beyond his skill and the first he knew about it was when it smashed into his jaw.

'Anyone have anything to say?' Spartacus glanced about, the camp which seemed to have become much busier. The armed guards were eager to look anywhere, as long as it wasn't at the ever more angry Spartacus, 'good then I'm going to find Plinius.'

'I'll come with you,' said Cassian.

'No, I'll go alone.' With that Spartacus turned on his heels and strode away, still seething inside. Orin roused and struggled to his feet, his head felt it was ready to crack open, he had never been hit so hard in his life.

'You're going to allow this, Father?'

'Allow it! ….Orin when you behave like this you shame me and you shame your people. Spartacus is not the man at fault here, for once learn from your mistakes and become a man like your brother Jacob.' Dara walked away from his son, shaking his head as he did so.

Spartacus searched for some time before he finally saw the familiar shape of Plinius, the young man sat on top of a large rock which in turn sat above a large gully. Spartacus was able to approach right up to Plinius' shoulder without him turning,

'You should take more heed of your surroundings Plinius these are dangerous lands.' The young man turned and smiled, and thankfully to Spartacus he looked more thoughtful than miserable.

'We have travelled together for what seems like a lifetime Spartacus, I know my friend when he approaches without the need to use my eyes.'

'What are you doing up here? It's cold come back to the camp fires.'

'Just thinking of Chia. I thought I heard her calling my name in the night, just hopeful thinking I suppose.'

'If you don't mind me saying Plinius, it was a mistake for you to come on this mission. Both you and Chia need time together, it only takes one of us to cut Flabinus' throat.'

'Would you have stayed at the fortress, while other men risked their lives.'

Spartacus laughed,

'Don't follow my example, that is a path that only leads to misery.' Plinius returned his laughter,

'What a life we have chosen, bloody fools.'

'Finally you are beginning to make sense.' Still laughing, he kicked a large rock into the gully causing a cascade of other boulders in response. The dislodgement stopped Spartacus and Plinius in their tracks, for where the rocks had been, a hand now reached towards the sky. The darkened hand stuck towards the heavens as if pleading with the Gods for rescue but it was evident to both men that whoever the hand belonged too, was far beyond saving. Spartacus scrabbled down into the gully sending other masonry tumbling down the slope, he recognised the clothing was similar to that worn by the villagers,

'Quickly fetch Cassian and best bring Dara too.'

At Spartacus' words Plinius burst into action without the weight of his armour he could move quickly, he had once took part in legionary races and he used all of that speed now. Spartacus in the mean time set about clearing the rubble and freeing the body to allow if possible the villagers to identify the man.

Plinius was some time, he had not realised that he had come so far on his early morning walk. At last he neared the spot where the body had been found. Cassian, Dara, Orin and many of the villagers had come to offer assistance. They were expecting to see one body, but were soon shocked to see no less than five within the gully. Spartacus had been busy, he had cleared the first body he had discovered, only to discover another body then another, until finally five pale white faces stared upwards, their misery still showing on their masks of death. Dara made his way down into the gully and brushed the dust from the nearest figure.

'You know these men?' Cassian asked Dara already knowing the answer by the visible anguish upon the old man's face. Dara nodded at first as though words would not easily come to him. 'These are men of our village, this is Jacob my son.' Dara wept clutching the lifeless form of his son close to his chest, Orin screamed his grief racing to be at his father's side. As he did other villagers rushed into the gully, old and young cried out their heart felt pain as they found a loved one. A mother tears in her eyes called,

'Meresh, where is Meresh?'

Orin answered Cassian's questioning look through his own sobs,

'There was a boy with these men no more than eight summers old.' Cassian and his men frantically searched the surrounding area, Plinius spotted a piece of cloth upon the far side of the gully. He walked over the cloth was bloodied but was too far from the other men to belong to them, as he turned to walk away, when something caught the corner of his eye, an object to the side of a large boulder. A small foot, so delicate and white against the dirt of the gully. Plinius investigated further and was soon bent over vomiting, and at that moment he wished he could erase his own mind for he knew no matter how long he lived, the sight before him would haunt his every slumber. Spartacus had seen Plinius vomiting and raced to his side,

'By the Gods, why-,' he could not finish his words. Even the old warrior who had seen many terrible things in his life, could not comprehend the savagery which had been inflicted upon the young boy. 'Plinius your cloak quickly, no mother should see this.' Plinius handed over his cloak readily and the both of them did their best to tidy the boy, wrapping his body so closely that the extent of his injuries were mostly hidden. Then Spartacus lifted the boy so gently, as if he was merely asleep not wishing to wake him, and carried him to his mother. The villagers carried their fallen family members back to their homes, as they did Cassian and his men held back not wanting to impose upon their grief.

'The boy he died the same way as the others?' Cassian asked of Spartacus.

He had seen the reaction of his two men and though the death of a boy is always sad these were hardened warriors used to such sights.

'No,' replied Spartacus. His next words were forced for he had no wish to have the image of the young boy's body within his mind. 'The boy had been totally destroyed but more than that, he

210

had been violated. This Flabinus and those that follow him are not men Cassian, they are beasts, wild animals we have to stop them. Cassian shocked by the boy's terrible fate, looked at his friend,

'We will, no matter the cost and the Gods know we have paid enough already, but we will see that man in the dirt and he will suffer. I was just going to kill the man, but i will bring to him pain, like the world has never known. If I fall Spartacus, promise me, you will do the same.'

'The promise is made, not one man here will rest until Flabinus is crying out his agony.'

The villagers took their time over preparing the dead for the ceremony, they wanted to say goodbye, Dara had arranged for the young boy to be tended by others from the village, rather than let his mother see the true extent of his injuries. As the ceremony and night moved along its sad path, there came a change in how Cassian and his men were treated. Before the dead villagers had been discovered, eyes shot out a mixture of mistrust and anger. Now it was replaced with sadness and a burning desire for retribution, which the villagers felt that Cassian and his men could deliver for them. This was made absolutely clear when Dara stood before his people,

'My friends, we have this day suffered great loss. We are a small community and five deaths will deliver grief to all of us, my friend Cassian warned us of the creature Flabinus and what acts he was capable. Some of us believed him, others chose to call the man liar simply because he is Roman. Up to this point I have never had reason to doubt Cassian or indeed the word of Flabinus, but it is clear we have done Cassian a great injustice and from this moment I intend to do all in my power to aid him in the capture and destruction of a man we once called friend. Each of you must search your hearts for the right course of action, you will take.'

As the ceremony proceeded Cassian and his comrades sat apart, but were visited by various members of the village, who came and offered apologies to each of them. Spartacus rose and went to the well, the sadness seemed to soak the very moisture from the air, as he drank a figure approached from behind.

'Spartacus if I may, I would like to speak with you though I know I do not deserve your time.'

'You may speak,' Spartacus replied. Surprised to see a very meek and timid Orin, standing before him.

'I owe you an apology, for I have wronged you. I let my feelings for everything roman cloud my judgement and it has cost

212

me more than I can bare, I encouraged Jacob to help Flabinus. Despite knowing my brother had misgivings about the man.'

'Firstly do not blame yourself for actions that were beyond your control, secondly if you hate Romans so much why trust Flabinus.'

'Flabinus is Thracian and hated the Romans.'

'Flabinus is no Thracian, I am Thracian and you should judge a man by his actions Orin not by the location of his birth. Nobody has more reason to hate Rome more than I, but in that man,' he pointed at Cassian 'you will find a man of great honour and humility, Roman or not he deserves your respect.'

Orin nodded his agreement and went to walk away but turned back to Spartacus,

'I do not deserve it, but I would like to call you friend.'

'We shall see, i only call men I respect friend, Orin.' At seeing Orin become even more crest fallen he added 'but it takes a braver man to admit he was wrong than one who goes for the blade to hide his stupidity, one day I believe we may well be friends, now go to your father for he needs you.' Spartacus watched Orin walk away and wondered if he had been wrong about the young man.

'Time will tell,' he said to himself.

Chapter XVII

The landing would be more trouble than it was worth for the small fishing boat, and so the figure decided he would wade into shore, his armour secured tightly in a bundle, he thanked those aboard and paid them handsomely for their trouble. He splashed down heavily into the water, and for a moment, feared he would lose his footing and with the weight of his armour bundle that could of spelt disaster. Melachus planted his feet firmly into the soft sand beneath the water's surface and began the arduous task of wading the short distance to the beach. Once there he waved to the fishing crew, then turned and wondered how long it had been since Cassian had set foot on this part of the shore. He trudged up to firmer ground, when something caught his eye, approximately two hundred paces further down the beach a figure lay motionless. The waves gently lapped at the man's legs but the figure offered no movement, and so Melachus moved towards him while still watching the surrounding area in case it was some elaborate trick. He reached towards the man, he grasped at him and flipped the figure over while watching for a hidden dagger being thrust towards him.

'Lathyrus.,Lathyrus answer me what happened?' Shock raced through Melachus body, terrible thoughts galloped through his mind that Cassian and even the great warrior Spartacus had been slain and all that remained was the forlorn figure before him. Lathyrus never answered Melachus' questions, his responses were just a series of grunts and murmurs, Melachus reached out and felt his forehead, the man was clearly suffering from a fever. The heavy frame of Lathyrus was dragged up the beach to where Melachus could build a small shelter to protect his patient from the midday sun. He gathered wood and made a fire, and then stripped Lathyrus of his clothes covering him with his own cloak. Doing what he could for the big man, but his medical knowledge was limited, and so contented himself with just keeping him warm and making him drink fresh water. Now and then Lathyrus grumblings would turn to rants, mostly inaudible but the occasional word like treachery could be clearly heard. All this only made Melachus more and more anxious with no hope of finding out the truth until Lathyrus' fever broke, if it broke. The rest of the day and following night were long, with Melachus unable to rest for watching over

215

his friend. Then thankfully in the early hours of the next morning, Lathyrus finally slipped into a more restful sleep. The following day Lathyrus hardly stirred at all, but his breathing had become easier and the pronounced sweating he had suffered the day before all but stopped. Melachus had found a number of injuries upon his friend including what were evidently dagger wounds to the thigh and side, he had done his best to dress and clean them. He wished Aegis and his special herbs were here to ensure Lathyrus was being well cared for. That day Lathyrus only woke briefly and although Melachus wanted to know so much he chose to allow his friend to regain his strength first, even though not knowing Cassian's fate was clawing at his insides.

Unaware of his friends plight, Cassian sat by the fire talking with Spartacus and Dara,

'From what I can determine we have two options available to us, Flabinus is restricted in the roads he may take.' Even though in his mind, he had decided on the route that he believed Flabinus would take, he felt less sure of himself these days and wanted to hear what the other two had to say.

'Surely he can go anywhere a vessel can take him, he has the wealth.' Spartacus replied.

'I don't think so, many Roman lands are blocked to him, some of the other lands receive too much influence from Rome and therefore the people there will gladly hand him over to gain favour. In my opinion he will either go across to Macedonia and try and avoid detection by the Roman forces there, and gradually work his way through the lands, up to the Germanic tribes. There he would be able to disappear and emerge when he so wished, I fear that if he reached that destination then we would have very little chance of tracking him down.'

'But you don't think he will head that way?' Dara asked, shrewdly reading the tone of Cassian and quickly understanding the young roman had other ideas.

'No, Flabinus is a planner. The route would leave too much to chance and too much of a risk, going through or close to so many Roman provinces.'

'So which way will he go?' asked Spartacus becoming impatient.

'Beyond Gaul across a great expanse of water lies a land which to the Roman people is almost legend. They say it is constantly covered by a mist, sailors tell tales, that vessels which enter the mist are rarely seen again. The stories include all manner of beasts

217

and of a population who emerge from the mist, naked and crying a terrible war chant, slaughtering all before them.'

'If this is so why would Flabinus go there?'

'Because like so many sailor tales, its complete rubbish. Tribes from Gaul have been trading with those people for decades maybe even longer, however they are a warlike people, we will need to be prepared. This will be a mission which will require a great deal more men and resources. Which is exactly what Flabinus will be doing now, he will sail close to the coast around Hispania, Gaul and cross over to the mystic land. Along the way he will gather men, ships and tribute, he will land there like a king and before long if we do not close upon him quickly he will have an army to carry out his demands.'

'Tell me Cassian why did Flabinus kill my son so close to the village.' Dara displayed the pain of losing his son for all to see. Cassian was slightly put off by the change in direction of the conversation, he stopped, looked at Dara and after careful consideration he answered.

'Because he wanted those bodies to be found, Flabinus has a deep hatred built into his very being. He does not understand the people of this village, and their wishes to live and stay together peaceably. Their lack of an ambition to expand their wealth and kingdom is foreign to him, and in his mind that is weakness. In you Dara he found a man who put his people first and was respected and trusted by those people in return. His act was a deliberate attempt at destroying the man, which he himself could never hope to be, no matter his intelligence or wealth. In short he wanted his act of murder and brutality to utterly destroy you, for you stand for everything that he despises.'

'What do you need to trap this man?' Dara asked, only a very slight twitch in the man's jaw, betrayed the anger that seethed beneath the calm exterior.

'Boats, supplies and men, most of all men,' Cassian replied.

'Many men of this village will wish to join you, and not just this village. Flabinus stole the wealth of many in this area with his deceit.'

'I need soldiers not farmers, this will be a dangerous and vicious affair if I know Flabinus.'

'Then you need men who will stand by your side, men who have chosen to offer up their lives for the task, not men who work for coin. Coin rarely glimmers so brightly when the blades begin to press.'

Dara's words landed heavily upon Cassian, it was true that he desperately needed men, and always considered that any man who volunteered to face danger to be worth more than one who was paid to do so.

'Very well Dara as you wish, send word to all those who would join us, Aegis and Tictus will travel to Utica and seek vessels, resources and men from my friend Critilo, in three weeks we shall set sail. Spartacus you and Plinius will train all that join us here, and Dara you will need to send to Cyrene, and purchase supplies to feed the training camp.' As Cassian finished speaking his friends nodded their agreement to his plans, but he glanced around the village watching the young men and wondered how many would not return. How would this village and the other surrounding villages just like it, survive without their brave sons who they sent off to war.

The following morning it was as though the village had suddenly woken from years in slumber, each inhabitant was rushing here and there, each trying to perform as many tasks as possible without taking breath. Aegis and Tictus rode of at sunrise, carrying with them signed papers from Cassian which he hoped would result in the materials he needed so badly being delivered to him. Spartacus and Plinius set about designing a training camp, so the farmers may at least learn to use a sword. All the villagers played their part, whether it was helping build temporary accommodation or gathering any spare supplies that they possessed. Orin and his mounted scouts were divided into pairs and sent off in different directions to carry the news to the various villages. Spartacus felt a familiar feeling which hadn't visited him for such a long time, years ago, just after the rebellion had started and the gladiators chose to band together rather than flee. They were joined by other slaves and gladiators who had escaped the many gladiatorial ludus from all over Roman provinces. Others who joined were poor Romans wishing for a better life, whatever the reason, the energy and enthusiasm was food to the soul and it enthralled Spartacus, and today he felt the same. The villagers looked taller and stronger and moved effortlessly no matter the task, the children helped where they could, no crying for attention. It was as though a mystical force had placed its hand upon each of them, and the sadness of just the last few days had been lifted from their shoulders. Spartacus glanced over many times in the direction of Cassian, who had made himself a makeshift desk, not inside a hut but in the centre of the village. He only raised his head to give instruction or send messengers upon their way. Organising people like a God, who would make the breeze dance through the branches of the trees. With just the slightest touch he could manipulate them to do his bidding. Dara moved amongst his people praising each of them only returning briefly to Cassian to receive more instructions, then darting off again. The first day ended, all the inhabitants drifted to their beds exhausted but happy. Spartacus would have forgiven them for a lacklustre start to the following morning. However, he learnt that these villagers were made of sterner stuff by the time he roused himself many had already completed tasks, which included preparing his morning meal. He and Plinius were consuming a meal as the first riders returned, and with them came other men who wished revenge upon Flabinus. However, not only warriors had come forward, other villagers came to help with the preparation, and brought valuable supplies with them. Spartacus could not believe the response and this by many who had little to give. Within little more than a day a quiet village had become a great cacophony of activity with Cassian sat at its centre directing, like a general plans a vast military campaign. Many of the scouts returned and were immediately sent off again, and then supplies arrived from Cyrene, the women of the village taking charge of the feeding the new arrivals.

'I wouldn't have thought it possible.' Spartacus remarked pausing for a moment next to Cassian.

'It's down to that man,' replied Cassian. He nodded towards Dara, 'the respect he commands in this province is frightening not just with his own people.'

'Not only him Cassian, another must take some credit.' Spartacus said no more but patted his friend on the shoulder as he walked back to his tasks. Cassian for his part sat back at Spartacus' words and for a moment allowed himself a small satisfied smile. So far it had been a wonderful achievement, whether they could actually carry this through to the end. He did not know the answer, but by the Gods they would give it go. He replaced the smile with his usual business like mask and returned to his planning,

'It's all in the detail,' he thought to himself, 'detail, detail, detail.'

Many miles to the north two other master planners were seated at a large imposing table, the table was adorned with the finery to be expected in such a wealthy area of Rome. The surroundings in stark contrast to the environment that the lowly villagers spent

223

their lives. Both men eyed each other, weighing up the man before them. It was rare for these two men to be in the same room let alone for the occasion to be so intimate.

'Tell me Crassus, now you have lost your wolf, will you leave my man be?'

'Oh things change Pompey you know that.'

Pompey reflected for a moment on Crassus' answer, for it could be clearly taken two ways. Either Crassus believed that Flabinus would somehow find his way back into the bosom of the senate, or he would perhaps rescind his call for Cassian to be eradicated.

'I believe we agreed that this meeting would be candid, Crassus?'

'Very well, plain speaking it is. Men in our position Pompey survive because other men fear us. If that fear lessens then we will lose our power to gain influence. I don't intend to allow that to happen.

'Then you insist on making an example of Cassian?'

'I expect Flabinus has already taken care of your bright young employee, my wolf as you call him can be extremely resourceful.'

'You should not under estimate Cassian, he can be more than a little resourceful himself. He may have had an extremely

224

successful political career in the senate, if he was inclined to do so. He certainly possesses the intelligence.'

'Intelligence,' scoffed Crassus, 'To survive in the senate, you require far more than intelligence.'

'That may be, but be warned Crassus. Cassian is likely to come to the conclusion that it makes no sense to wait for your assassins to continuously attempt to kill him. The bright young man may decide to take the head from the beast.'

'Then I best be quick, as you should be, for my influence grows.'

Pompey laughed,

'Oh Crassus, you must learn to take to the field and win victories. For until you do you are just a trader, and Rome is reluctant to have a trader as Emperor.'

Crassus flushed with anger, no matter how many successes he gained or influence he gathered, it all came down to his lack of military victories. Made all the worse, because his opponent Pompey seemed to have such a skill on the battlefield. Failing for once to find the words to argue, Crassus simply stood, and strode from the room without looking back. Pompey watched the man leave, it was a small victory but a victory none the less. It was a pity for young Cassian, Crassus was determined to see him slain and with his coin eventually he would get his way. Pompey raised his goblet of wine and offered a small prayer for Cassian, in the great scheme of things Cassian was not important to his plans, but the man had served him well and as such deserved to be honoured.

Chapter XVIII

Upon the coast a small makeshift shelter stood against the firm breeze which gathered its momentum across the water, and then rushed inland. Inside a dozing Melachus could not hold back the weariness anymore, and had drifted away as the sun had disappeared the previous day. Still seated, he had fallen to sleep while keeping a close eye on Lathyrus, fearing his condition should worsen. Therefore slipping back to how it had been when he had first discovered the man face down in the sand. A sudden slap in the face made him jump, waking instantly his hand moving to the dagger within his belt. The slap had come from a empty water skin now lying stationary within his lap,

'Water, you give water to a dying man. What's wrong with wine lad?'

'Lathyrus your awake,' replied Melachus shocked by his friend's sudden emergence from slumber.

'By the Gods lad your quick, I understand why Dido promoted you now.'

'Bollocks! What happened, where is Cassian?'

'Couldn't tell you, I was left with the ship to help the crew, them being rather short of men that is.'

'Why are they short of men? It was a full crew when I left.'

'Mutiny all but eight of them tried to cut our throats, it was us or them. It was us that Neptune smiled upon and our enemies either died where they stood or chose to go over the side and take their chances against the waves.'

'But if the mutiny failed why are you here?' Melachus shook his head as he spoke totally bemused by the whole thing.

'Cassian and the others were put ashore not far from this very spot, and I was asked to accompany the reduced crew further up the coast. On the following night I had quite a few skins of wine and so retired early but later that night I was woken by talking further down the deck. They did not realise at first I was within the shadows listening every word that was spoken, it seems this little band were working for Flabinus all along, he had planted them on the most obvious vessel to set off after him. It is obvious that Cassian is not the only clever bastard. Anyway eventually they became aware they were not alone, and they came at me. I know I put two of them down but they were armed and I was not and I chose to go over the side before they did for me completely. The bastards stuck me well enough a couple of times though, and they searched for me, in the end I think they believed me drown. So I swam for shore, after that it becomes a little blurred, you probably know more than I do.

'It's pure luck I found you, dragged you up here and did my best.'

'That's not true is it?'

'What do you mean?' Replied Melachus his temper nearly getting the better of him.

'Well I can't smell food yet.' Lathyrus boomed with laughter. Melachus began to laugh but then held his finger to his lips, he pulled the dagger from his belt and passed it to Lathyrus. Then slowly he took his sword from the far side of Lathyrus and slowly moved to look around the side of the makeshift shelter. Riders were moving towards them with pace, and numbered at least twenty, far too many for Melachus to fight.

'We may be in trouble Lathyrus.'

'Aren't we always?' He sat up without too much trouble and stared at the riders approaching them, 'stick your chest out and talk like you own the place, if we are going to die let's do it with some pride.'

The riders stopped just short of the shelter and hailed those inside, Lathyrus made to rise but Melachus prevented him from doing so,

'No stay here, I will see what they want.' Melachus rose from his position and placed his sword into his belt, gulped down a fresh intake of air and then walked into the sunshine. A rider at the front of the group did not waste time with pleasantries,

'Who are you and what are you doing in our lands?'

'My name is Melachus and I have an injured man inside,' Melachus nodded towards the shelter as he spoke. 'We are in search of our friend Cassian.'

'If you are friends with Cassian, please consider us friends too, but if you lie and wish harm to him then you will never leave these shores, is your injured friend able to ride?'

'If the journey is not too far I believe so, and may I have your name.'

'My name is Orin, I was carrying out some requests for Cassian but no doubt you can discuss that, with the man yourself.' Two of Orin's men gave up their own horses and helped Lathyrus aboard one of the steeds. They in turn doubled up on backs of their friends mounts, and the party moved away, despite Orin's coldness towards Melachus he noticed that the young leader kept the pace down and Melachus could only imagine this was to aid Lathyrus.

At the same time that Orin arrived at the makeshift shelter of Melachus, Aegis awoke from a disturbed sleep. The figure that had haunted his slumber for so many nights had finally revealed itself to him, and as it did so it stood so proud next to Flabinus. The shock of it had woken Aegis he could not believe he hadn't recognised the young man earlier. But not only the young man, but also the features shared between him and the older Flabinus. Aegis grew angry, they would have had the leverage to bring Flabinus to his knees and he foolishly had not recognised the opportunity, he cursed his own old age. He kicked out sending pots hurtling from the hut and beat his own forehead, Spartacus entered the hut quickly, blade drawn thinking Aegis under attack for he had never heard the old warrior curse unless in battle. Shocked by the sight of Aegis chastising himself he tried to calm his old friend,

'Aegis, steady yourself what is wrong?' Spartacus asked, placing a hand on Aegis' shoulder.

'We had him, and now where is he? It's all my fault.'

'What is? What has happened?' As Spartacus replied, Cassian joined them in the hut.

'What's going on?' He echoed Spartacus' request to know what troubled Aegis.

'The boy it was him, and I didn't see it.'

'Who? what boy?' Again Cassian asked, becoming frustrated.

'Dion, forgive me Cassian I have only just put a face to my visions. He was the young man I saw at Flabinus' camp.'

'If you are correct Aegis we must try and warn Lathyrus, if Dion is a traitor then there is a chance that all the men we spared that night on the vessel are in his employ, this is not something to torture yourself about Aegis.'

'You don't understand Cassian, when finally I saw them side by side in my vision, it was so very clear.'

'Aegis tell us,' demanded Spartacus beginning to lose patience.

'Dion is kin to Flabinus, maybe son or younger brother but there is no doubt.'

'And we had him,' Spartacus gasped, shocked at the revelation.

'We still might, he is unaware that we have this information. As far as he is concerned we are blissfully ignorant of his true identity.'

'He would make an impressive bargaining tool.' Spartacus smirked as he spoke.

'No! Spartacus as you are aware I like to make deals, but Dion has chosen the same path as Flabinus and for those that have done so, there will be no compromise, if we have Dion I will personally deliver his head to Flabinus before I take his.' Spartacus stared at Cassian, he knew it made sense to hold Dion to try and gain advantage over Flabinus, but the more he stared into those eyes so determined to exact revenge he also knew it had long passed the stage of making sense. Flabinus and his supporters would be wiped from this world, the usual rules of engagement had been swept aside.

'Very well,' replied Spartacus nodding his head in agreement.

'If you would Spartacus, when Orin returns allow him time to rest and then find Dion and the vessel, dispatch the others but bring Dion back to me.' Spartacus again nodded his agreement, now was not the time for conversation.

The day was nearing its end as Orin and his riders entered the village with two new guests. Cassian and his men heard the tale of how Melachus returned , and how he found Lathyrus wounded upon the beach. Any doubts Spartacus had about the chosen path of Cassian and his attitude towards what must be done about Dion, seemed to evaporate. It was clear that Dion was just as deceitful as his older family member, and if he intended playing a man's game he must accept all the consequences of that game. The riders were bathed and fed, then Cassian proceeded to give them their new orders. Spartacus expected Orin to raise issue with the fact that he would not lead this mission, but he simply nodded his agreement and even arranged for Spartacus to find garments more in keeping with the local population. As the sun began its final journey beyond the hills, Spartacus, Orin and twelve other men set out, if Dion had stuck to the location given to him by Cassian then he would be easy to find. Spartacus hoped that finding the vessel would indeed be simple, as for getting aboard Dion did not know about the visions of Aegis or the fact that Lathyrus still lived. Therefore he should have no suspicions about the task Spartacus must carry out. Time passed giving Spartacus ample opportunity to speak with Orin and the men, the background to each was one of hardship. Since Cyrene had become a Roman province the trials suffered by each of them had multiplied, it seems that Roman influence had chosen to spread discord amongst its once content population, no doubt issues made far worse by the meddling of Flabinus. The reason why the Roman authorities had taken such an action was simple in Spartacus' mind, when the local population cannot agree amongst themselves then any coordinated rebellion was made almost impossible.

Eventually the talking stopped as it always did before the most dangerous part of the mission began, no matter how hardened the warrior, thoughts would inevitably drift to those loved ones left behind, and Spartacus was no different to any other man in this respect. He allowed his mind to drift away, his mind focusing on the faces of both wife and child. He wondered to himself what Cynna was doing now, the pain of the separation dug into his very being, its sharpness the match for any blade.

As if connected by some invisible thread that wove beyond the distant horizon, traversing hills, valleys and raging rivers seeking a lover in a distant land. Cynna gazed from the old fortress walls as if willing the familiar shape of Spartacus to appear upon the road, he would approach as he always did, firstly acknowledging her with a brief wave and then as he drew close the head would drop to the side and a nervous smile would spread upon his face. No matter how long the two had been with one another, upon every return it was the same, they would be consumed with the feelings of two young lovers timid at showing the emotions which burned so deeply within. That was until they reached their chambers, she caught herself smiling at her own thoughts, a slight scarlet colouring appearing upon her cheeks. She glanced around anxious that maybe a passing guard could somehow see into her mind. She looked once again to the horizon and resigned herself that her lover would not appear that night,

'Night my love, hurry home,' she said quietly and slowly moved away.

Despite her resignation to another night without Spartacus, before entering her quarters she could not help glancing over the fortress walls. As she quietly opened her door she could hear the two sets of tears which had become second place each night. Flora and Chia both cried themselves to sleep, Cynna powerless to help them in their sadness closed her door to be alone with her own.

Chapter XIX

Spartacus watched as the night fell and the majority of the torches went out on the vessel down in the small cove. Orin silently crawled alongside Spartacus, he was extremely careful not to make a sound, although in truth the vessel was still some distance away.

'Do we go in tonight?'

'No we wait till first light, they will more than likely send men ashore to do a little hunting. We don't want to scare them off before they realise we are friends.' Spartacus smiled as he spoke, and wondered about the abilities of those men he now commanded.

'When we board do kill them all?' asked Orin. His wish for vengeance no matter how small, evident upon his face.

'All but one of them, him we take back to Cassian, I will make it clear which one he is.' For quite some time Spartacus watched the gentle lapping of the waves as the pounded the small rocks beneath them but eventually sleep overtook him. Orin had posted a guard who would in turn be relieved some time later and so be able to catch some rest before they attempted to fulfil their mission. In the morning Orin nudged Spartacus awake,

'You were right, looks like at least four of them are coming ashore.'

'Right pull the men in closer,' Spartacus waited for all of the men to be within a distance which would allow him to talk at a low whisper. 'Listen, those men are our target they serve a man who killed the men of the village. Within the ranks of Flabinus there are no people who just work for pay, they believe in the man and eagerly do his bidding. All die except for one, whom I will point out to you. I will go down first and then hail you to join me, at first we will be friendly and give them no cause for concern.'

'And when do we stop being friendly?' asked one of the men.

'Oh, you will know believe me, but keep your hands away from your weapons. These are Flabinus' men they deal in deceit and will be alert to any sign, understand?'

The men nodded and so Spartacus began his dissent down into the cove, keen to place himself between those who had come ashore and the water's edge. He picked his way towards the small group getting within twenty paces before they noticed them,

'You need to be more aware of what's around you Dion, if I was an enemy you would already be dead.' The man to his front jumped at the sudden appearance of the muscled warrior. For just a moment it looked as though he would draw his weapon, but then his body relaxed and his hand dropped back to his side.

'Spartacus, where is Cassian?' replied Dion. Trying to hide his embarrassment at being taken by surprise.

'He sent me ahead with some more recruits to help sail the vessel,' as he did so he placed his arm around Dion's shoulder 'and where is that old rogue Lathyrus?'

'That I cannot tell you Spartacus, one morning I awoke to find him gone, he had spoken badly of Cassian for making him stay behind. I fear he may have slipped over the side letting his annoyance prevail and sought his fortunes elsewhere.'

'It's possible Lathyrus is run by emotions and rarely uses his head.'

Up on the rocks Orin and his men saw Spartacus be place a hand on the figure's shoulder and knew this was the man so eagerly awaited by Cassian. Then a short time later Spartacus waved for them to join him and as they made their way down, he continued to speak with Dion,

'Now this lot we picked up in Cyrene not what I would call first rate soldiers or sailors but they will do. They will be at your command once we are aboard, but you may have to give them some instruction, and if any give you any trouble then do not hesitate to throw them overboard.

'Of course that won't be a problem,' replied Dion, he gave a sickening sweet smile.

'Let's get back to the vessel I'm famished, and we have managed to get hold of some rather nice wine in Cyrene too, what do you say?'

Dion once again smiled at Spartacus' words, and led the way back towards the surf. It wasn't long before all of them stood on the deck gazing around at the condition of the vessel. 'You have done well Dion, I'm no expert when it comes to sailing but it looks like everything is in good order.'

'Thank you Spartacus, the men have done well.'

'Yes the vessel looks good, it's just a shame you are such a traitorous little bastard.' Before Dion could react Spartacus' massive fist connected with his jaw and for the young man the world turned to darkness. The sailors all died within a heart beat as Orin's men took advantage of their shock and hesitation. The

240

battle for the vessel was one sided and brief, with men of the villagers moving quickly about their task.

'Well done, over the side with those scum and Orin if you could secure our little friend here, I think we will eat before returning back to the village.' Spartacus was impressed with the speed and efficiency in which the villagers had gone about the task of disposing of the enemy, clearly they were not simple farmers who did not know one end of a blade from another. He congratulated Orin on the skills of his men and also told them as a group, which he hoped would go some way to repairing some of the poor relations that Cassian's men and the villagers had suffered in the past. A meal was heartily eaten and it wasn't until the group were preparing to leave that the battered Dion began to stir, as Orin walked past the man he simply struck him with the pommel of his sword sending the man back into slumber.

Cassian awaited the return of Spartacus eagerly, he wondered what he would do when faced with the kin of Flabinus. Usually the level headed Cassian would not blame a person for simply being related to such a man, but when the family member joins in his actions he becomes complicit in them. Dara strolled up to Cassian, though in truth he had been observing the Roman for quite some time,

'The weight of leadership weighs heavily upon you this day Cassian.'

'No more than you have had to bare, my friend.'

'You wonder what actions you will take, if Spartacus is successful and brings this Dion back to the village. You should not worry the correct course will take place.'

'Spartacus will succeed he always does, and as a group we decided all these men will die, but am I acting for justice or vengeance?' The anxiety of the situation of what to do with Dion obviously playing upon his mind.

'I believe in this case they are one of the same, besides when that man is brought into this village you will be lucky if the villagers don't rip him limb from limb.'

'Man…… Dara he is little more than a boy.'

'Cassian he chose his path, he chose to act like a beast. If a young wolf tries to rip out your throat you don't allow him to do so because of its age, you slaughter it and be grateful it is gone from this world before it is grown to full size. But maybe you should try and question him, any information we can learn may prove useful, failing that just kill the whelp and put him from your mind.' As Dara finished speaking the scouts to the north hailed that riders were approaching the village. 'Looks as though your man has completed his task, let's see what this young killer has to say.'

Spartacus manoeuvred his small band of riders into the centre of the village, where Orin unceremoniously tipped the bruised Dion onto the sun baked ground. Cassian approached the figure, but initially did not speak merely looked into the young man's eyes. He circled Dion, who had only just managed to regain his feet but at all times turned to keep Cassian in view.

'You failed in your attempt to kill Lathyrus,' Cassian spoke quietly and with confidence to see if his words betrayed any emotional upon Dion's face. The captive simply stared back the news that an intended victim had escaped seemed not to perturb him. 'So the question is, Dion is what do we do with you?'

'No! The question Cassian, is what will my brother do to you, your men and your families if I am harmed in any way.' His words made Plinius draw his weapon, Cassian held the young warrior back.

'You have great confidence in your brother's ability, but this time I feel it is misplaced.'

243

'Whatever you do to me, I will not talk Cassian I will not give up my brother's plan to you.'

'You misunderstand as to the reason you were brought here,' Cassian smiled, 'you were brought before me for the crimes you have committed, and those you ordered those that followed you to commit.' Just a flicker of anxiety appeared within Dion's face, this is not what he expected. Dion managed to puff out his chest,

'You think you can scare me in to giving you information?'

'Oh I am sure you are brave Dion and you will need to be, punishment is death. The execution will be carried out at first light tomorrow. Plinius if you would secure the prisoner within one of the huts.'

'It will be a pleasure,' he replied. Lifting Dion by his scalp, Plinius wrenched the young man to his feet, as they crossed the square he whispered in the captive's ear. 'You and your brother have undervalued the man in which you have declared war upon, tomorrow you will die and your brother, no matter how long it takes will follow your path.'

'You think I am afraid to die, kill me and you lose your edge, and trust me you will need all the advantage you can get.'

'You really don't understand do you, the crimes your brother has committed has removed any chance of negotiation, and as one of his men your fate is sealed.'

'Killing me would make no sense,' Dion replied. A slight tremor now could be heard within his voice.

'Sense, these people do not require things to make sense. The man you have just spoken to has lost his wife, these villagers have lost loved ones. Your brother himself killed my best friend who was trying to save those he cared for, do you think for one moment any of us want to make sense of what has happened? No! We just want to rip you all to pieces, and do you know, it doesn't make a difference how many of us die doing so, we will wipe the house of Flabinus from this world, and in such a short time nobody will remember it even existed.

'My brother......'

'Your brother what? He is already a hunted man in every Roman province in the known world, most of his men are already dead. He scrabbles to a safe place, but he knows we are coming no matter what traps he lays for us, we just keep on coming. The only question left to ask which one of us will take his head from his shoulders.'

'And you think you could, do you? Dion scoffed at the idea.

'Look at those men,' Plinius pulled Dion's head around to face Cassian, Aegis and Spartacus. 'Each one of those men fought in the games in Utica and defeated their champions. Aegis lost his hand and still crushed the skull of his enemy. Cassian fights like a ghost deceptive in all his moves and then there is Spartacus, the finest warrior I have ever seen. If your brother faces Cassian or Aegis he will need all the Gods to be working for him to survive, but if he meets Spartacus, then the Gods won't be enough.' With that Plinius threw Dion into the hut and secured tightly to the beams, and with one last look at the young man before him turned and closed the door. The darkness closed around Dion, and the fear took him and quietly, secretly he cursed his brother.

Spartacus informed Cassian of how the mission went, and of the qualities that Orin and his men had shown.

'You know the information I require,' replied Cassian when Spartacus finished his report.

'I do.'

'Then tell me Spartacus, have they got what it takes.'

'You ask me to make an impossible judgement Cassian. Each of the men sent on that mission performed their task with speed and efficiency, and killed with skill. However you must remember that they not only had numbers on their side but also the element of surprise. Who knows what they will be like when the challenges of the task ahead of us test them, they will unlikely have such an advantage over the enemy and I do not know how they will react. Cassian looked crestfallen at Spartacus' words, he had hoped for a more enthusiastic response from the veteran warrior before him. Spartacus was aware that he did not bring comfort to his friend and so added,

'It was not so long ago, that I knew a member of the pampered Roman elite. If someone had asked me then if he could be a warrior, I would have answered that he would probably have the fighting prowess of an old woman. I would have been wrong Cassian, your skills have proven that to me. You can train a soldier, give him the finest weapons and the endless drill until he moves without thinking to the orders received. You must understand however, that true warriors are born not created Cassian. All we can hope is that within that group of men, there will be a number of real warriors. The remainder that are not blessed with such skill will do their best, and try not to die too quickly.'

Chapter XX

There was a spring in the step of most of the villagers, capturing the brother of Flabinus helped go some way to dispelling the myth of the man. It did not seem possible but those that had arrived to fight became more intent upon their training. Where those men responsible for preparation doubled their efforts, especially when it came to helping Cassian and his men. It seemed a lifetime ago when these same people treated Cassian with mistrust, gone was the ill feeling, banished from each of their hearts. Roman, Greek, Thracian or Judean it did not matter, all were united in the pursuit and destruction of Flabinus and his men.

Night fell and in time the village stepped into another world of slumber, what had been a hive of activity just a few hours before, now lay motionless beneath the eerie blue light of the moon. The village appeared deserted with the exception of a dosing sentry upon an old rickety stool, his back supported by the hut wall which housed his captive.

'You are up late Nechama,' said the guard. He forced himself to be more awake than he felt, for Nechama was a widow and a fine looking one at that, it would not hurt to impress her.

'Yes, to be honest Dara asked me to bring food and water to the prisoner but with so much happening I forgot all about it.'

'Let the bastard starve.'

'I do not do it for his sake, I merely wish to fulfil Dara' wishes. At least the task gave me the opportunity to bring you some nice wine,' as she raised a goblet.

'Very well but stay in the light and do not release his bonds,' replied the guard. He hungrily took the wine, sending it down his gullet in one quick motion.

She nodded her agreement and when the guard opened the door she slipped silently inside allowing her eyes to become accustomed to the poorly lit room. For his part the guard took to his stool once again, for some reason tiredness rushing over him. He fought valiantly to remain alert but within moments his eyes were closed and a deep rumbling snore erupted from his slumped figure.

The man before her was tied to the beams of the hut, he stirred as he felt the presence of another person within the room,

'Who is there,' he croaked.

249

It had been some time since liquid had passed his lips, coupled with the natural anxiety he felt at the position he found himself in, it was not surprising his mouth was as dry as the desert. At first Nechama did not speak, she merely observed the man from distance but eventually, timidly she moved closer,

'You have nothing to fear from me, I have been instructed to bring you refreshment.'

She moved in close to him and held a goblet of water to his lips which he rushed to take. The cooling liquid spilled down his parched throat. She took a cloth and wiped the splashed water from his tunic.

'Your very kind,' he spoke quietly not wanting to alert the guard.

'I merely do as my village elder asks.'

'I am sure your husband would not want you so close to me.'

'My husband died many summers ago, it is a pleasant change to serve a man his meal,' as she spoke she raised chicken to his mouth. Which he hungrily feasted upon, bits of the roasted bird came away falling upon his person and floor.

'I could more easily manage if my bonds were loosened, I'm better when my hands are free to do as they wish,' he smiled at her,

250

making sure she understood his intention. He was sure he saw her blush though it was difficult in this light, he thought to himself that this is the opportunity soon he will be leaving this place. More food was raised to his mouth but as he opened to accept, this time a dagger pressed against his throat and a cloth quickly inserted between his teeth, forcing his tongue downwards preventing him from making more than just a grunt.

'I need to speak with you, and honesty would be the best policy.' Nechama stared intently at the man as she spoke, her eyes burned with determined fire. He was left in no doubt that she would draw the cold metal across his throat if he displeased her, he nodded his compliance. His mind raced over the possible intentions of the woman, just moments ago he thought he may have a chance of freedom but now he stared at her in utter confusion.

'Your brother, when did he decide to kill the men from the village?' As she spoke she removed the cloth from his mouth but applied slightly more pressure to the blade to act as a warning that he should not raise the alarm.

'My brother did not involve me in the preparation in his plan's, he is always secretive even where I am concerned.'

'So why kill them?' she persisted, pressing the blade.

'Why not? I cannot understand my brother's ways or methods, I was not born with his genius. However if they needed to die for my brother's plans to work then die they must.'

'You still honour him, though his actions will forfeit your life?'

'I am not yet dead and yes I honour him he is a great man, so what if a few farmers die along the way. When a general wins lands and slaves few mention the soldiers that die in the battles. Besides there is no need for me to die you could cut these bonds.' She ignored his last words for a moment looking straight into his eyes, she seemed to be losing the calm exterior she had managed so far to portray since entering the hut.

'What about the boy?'

'What boy?' replied Dion, at a loss to what she was talking about.

'My son was with the men of the village who Flabinus slaughtered, why Dion?' For the first time Dion came to realise just how much danger he was in, he tried to pull at the bonds but they had been far too expertly tied.

'I am not responsible for my brother's actions,' he cried.

'Do you know what he did to my son?' As she spoke she wiped the tears from her eyes which now came freely. 'Dara tried to keep his injuries from me, but I crept into the hut while the other women feasted. Your brother destroyed my son, he wasn't even half your age and yet Flabinus showed no mercy.' Dion went to speak but Nechama thrust the cloth back into his mouth, 'be quiet I need to think.' She turned and walked a few paces away from Dion, she seemed to be rocking as though trying to shake the grief from her soul. Finally she turned and stared at Dion,

'He would have cried for me, but your brother stopped his cries for his mother. Placed his hand over my son's mouth cutting of the air and therefore any chance of help reaching him. Very like you Dion nobody heard my son's final moments, I doubt I have the same skills as your brother but I will do my best.' She raised the dagger as she finished talking and walked towards Dion. The man before her struggled with his bonds and tried to scream, but the noise was muffled and the only person who may have heard him was the guard who sat slumped upon his stool. The wine goblet was perched upon the ground next to him, if the guard had been more of an expert when it came to wine he may well of thought that it tasted bitter. The drug it possessed would not harm him,

253

merely make him sleep and oblivious to the agony which was being experienced just a few paces away. The night wore on, one man slept as another bled.

Spartacus, Cassian and Dara had taken to strolling the village early in the day it gave them the chance to go over the plans for the coming days without the chaos of the now busy village. Suddenly Spartacus stopped in his tracks,

'Your man's asleep Dara, excellent guard he is.'

'He's a good man, I don't understand.' The confusion on Dara's face made the other two quicken their pace until finally Spartacus burst into a sprint. He reached the guard and tried shaking him awake, when he got no response he picked up the goblet and smelt it's contents,

'Drugged, he's alive but I guess will not wake for some time,' on saying this, he steadily moved towards the door of the hut.

'Be careful Spartacus, he may still be in there.'

'I doubt it, Dion will be long gone.' Spartacus replied. He threw back the door while drawing his own dagger just to be sure. Horror met his eyes the insides of the hut now resembled a slaughter house.

'By the Gods,' the words escaping from Cassian's lips as he appeared at Spartacus' shoulder. For a moment the three stood there, transfixed by the scene not wanting to move into the hut but eventually Spartacus closed on the carcass of Dion. He soon realised that most of the wounds upon the dead man resembled those that had been inflicted upon the young boy from the village. He scanned the hut looking for clues to who had carried out this act and there in the shadows of the hut, a figure sat slumped against the wall. He gestured to Dara who approached the figure,

'Nechama,' he said. No reply came and as he bent down he realised that she was covered in blood and not only that of Dion. For after taking her revenge she had sat herself against the wall and dragged the sharp blade across her wrist, blood and grief spilled from her to rest on the dusty hut floor. 'Oh no! Nechama...Nechama.' Dara could still see where her tears had rolled down her face, he closed her eyes and pulled her head close to his chest. He sobbed unashamed. Stroking her hair and cradling her like a child who was going to sleep, and in her ear he whispered,

'Forgive me Nechama, the fault is mine I should never have allowed those men into the village. My poor Nechama, your pain has gone now. Be with your son, no more pain, no more pain.'

Before most of the villagers woke Nechama's body was removed from the hut and dressed in a new tunic. Spartacus and Cassian remained at the hut, not wanting anyone to witness the carnage inside.

'I best get rid of the body,' Spartacus said.

'I require something from it first,' Cassian replied. Spartacus looked at Cassian confusion within his mind, what could Cassian want from Dion's mutilated corpse. He was going to leave it and not enquire but he felt he had to ask the question,

'What could you possibly want?'

'I will tell you Spartacus but I think it best we keep it secret from the rest of the men, they may not understand. When finally we face Flabinus we need something that will shake his confidence, perhaps force him to act out of character and make mistakes. That's why I intend to drop his brother's head in his lap, if the man is capable of feeling anything then that should unsettle the bastard.' Cassian spoke as though expecting Spartacus to react angrily to such an action, as though it went against some unwritten code, but he just looked thoughtful as if weighing up the plan.

'All things considered, I believe it is worth the attempt,' Spartacus finally replied.

'I thought you would try and dissuade me from the task.'

'As you know Cassian I have committed many acts that I am not proud, but I like to think that in all my actions I have been justified, but expect Flabinus will offer such excuses for in own actions too.'

'You are nothing like Flabinus, in your darkest moments you will question your actions, that is what makes you human, what makes you a man. Flabinus is too filled with self importance to think in such a way, the people he slaughters are beneath him, like vermin.

'Thank you Cassian, but I expect to some out there I am no better than Flabinus.'

'Then they are wrong Spartacus,' replied Cassian.

An uneasy silence settled upon the two and both were grateful when Tictus rushed up to them, he tried to speak but a mixture of trying to catch his breath because of his running and the smile upon his face made it awkward to catch his words.

'Calm down Tictus, what is it?' asked Cassian, fearing some unknown disaster.

'The…..the vessels from Critillo, they have been spotted they will make land fall before the sun goes down.

'Thank the Gods, I could only hope that he would be able to keep his promises, moods and opinions change so much in Rome,' he clasped Spartacus by both shoulders, ' but we will have Flabinus now, we will have him.'

Cassian scuttled of with Tictus to make preparation to transfer the supplies to the vessels, which would soon be landing. Spartacus was left staring after them, he glanced into the hut and then back at the departing figure of Cassian. Obviously Cassian had momentarily about the hanging corpse of Dion within the hut.

'Bloody marvellous,' he said to himself. Then took the long dagger from his tunic and walked into the eerie darkness of the hut.

Chapter XXI

As the next few days passed all the inhabitants of the village again busied themselves with the tasks that needed completing, before the men could leave to bring Flabinus to justice. Since the death of Nechama a strange melancholy had settled upon each and every one of them. They regarded her as yet another innocent, whose life had been destroyed by the actions of a cruel and despicable man. The enthusiasm which had beset the village only a few days before had evaporated to be replaced by a grim determination to complete the task ahead, even the children seemed to smile less, laughter becoming a distant memory. Critillo had provided three vessels, which settled alongside the one already in Cassian's possession. In addition Cassian's friend had also sent the men to man the vessels and supplies for a long journey aboard ship. To Cassian's surprise though also made available to him were a hundred fighting men, though they wore no insignia. Obviously the various politics within Rome was reason behind this, however it was still blatantly clear these were men of the legions. They answered an order with perfect efficiency and had been given clear

259

instruction that Cassian would be their officer, a strange concept to both Cassian and the men.

The day when the fleet would set sail was fast approaching and although Cassian outwardly seemed calm and assured, inside his stomach churned with worry. Fearing that he had missed some vital preparation, which would come back to haunt his men. He raised these concerns with Spartacus the night before they would put to sea,

'Spartacus go over these lists I have made I don't want to have missed anything.'

'Unlikely Cassian, and besides what we haven't got now, we can do without. No campaign is perfect,' replied Spartacus.

'I would rather any plans I have made will be as close to perfect as possible. I do not wish men to die because of my error.'

'No matter how well you plan, men will die on this voyage. Try to avoid any unnecessary deaths but expect them all the same. It's an occupational hazard I'm afraid with soldiers and war. Besides to a general all soldiers are mere numbers, don't throw them away recklessly but you must be prepared to take risks.'

'Many of these men are not soldiers Spartacus,' replied Cassian.

'Yes they are, from this point they have chosen to fight. You have to get out of you head that many of these men are mere farmers or indeed friends. We have a task to complete, each man will be subject to military discipline and each man is expendable, no matter who they are.'

'No matter who?'

'This is not a game Cassian, if you think you can create your plans and just tick them off like some warehouse manifest you're sadly misguided. Flabinus is a maniac that is not in question but he is resourceful, devious and highly intelligent. We will be lucky if any of us return, and so you must not get too protective of the men. You need to be thinking clearly at all times and fretting over those that have died will not help those that still live.'

'I just wish that I could meet this Flabinus face to face, and that would put an end to it,' Cassian replied, shaking his head at the enormity of the task.

'Be careful for what you wish for, the man has skill. He bested Bull easily and that was no simple matter.'

'A good man Bull.'

'One of the best, and sorely missed. There is no doubt I would prefer to have the old rogue with us, upon this journey.

Time passed, farewells were uttered and the time had begun for Cassian to start his campaign. The strong breeze whipped across the water and when it collided with the heavy wooden planks it shot upwards and across the deck. It struck the chiselled features of Spartacus as he watched the shore line disappearing beyond the horizon. Travelling by boat had never been high on his list of favourite past times, and already his old feelings of discomfort came flooding back. It was all too enclosed, each footing was less sure than it would have been on land and men's fates at sea, were always at the whim of the Gods. It seemed while on the water, celestial beings were far more likely to be in a playful mood. The air too annoyed him, each breathe tasted heavily of salt, he spat the rancid taste from his mouth and then cursed as the breeze brought his spittle flying back to him, colliding with his tunic. He surveyed his surroundings, three other vessels travelling the same path as the one he occupied, each crammed with supplies, weapons and men. Each and every man keen on removing Flabinus' head from his neck, Spartacus wondered if the man knew or even cared about the loathing he nurtured in others. This was just a small sample of the masses who would happily strike him down and yet the man still lived. Cassian had told Spartacus in some lengths of all the crimes that were believed to have been carried out by Flabinus, or upon his orders. Amongst his victims were not only the poor, farmers and merchants, many of his victims belonged to the eminent houses of Rome, and the royal family members in more than one state around the known world. If they were not careful they would all stampede themselves to death in the rush to kill him. Cassian and Lathyrus now approached, the latter holding out a goblet of wine.

'Thank you Lathyrus, how long will I have to stay on this wreck?'

'The journey will take some time, most of it in waters that I know well, the last quarter of the journey I'm afraid will be educated guess work,' the old sailor replied.

'We hope to find a scout willing to cross to this mysterious land, once we get to the northern lands of Gaul,' informed Cassian.

'Surely we will not be aboard this floating casket all that time?'

'No,' laughed Lathyrus, 'we shall embrace this coast up beyond Utica, from there we will sail around Hispania and then follow the coast of Gaul to our destination. We won't be stopping at major ports. But along the journey, there are a number of safe harbours big enough to take our fleet where we can re-supply and let you land lovers feel the earth beneath your feet.'

'Thank the Gods, and may they bring land swiftly to my bloody feet. Already my insides yearn for solid footing, they churn at the movement of this bloody barge.'

The days and nights disappeared into the past, the Gods sometimes sent calm seas which grated the men's nerves as progress became laboured and then at other times they sent ferocious storms which battered the small convoy of ships. Men were lost in the storms, for many aboard the transports were not sailors. The great waves plucked them from safety taking them to a watery oblivion, but the convoy forced its way through the storms ever onwards. Utica came and then disappeared from view, then the coast of Hispania provided a few enjoyable resting places. However they were all too brief and the flotilla moved on, keen not to be late for its destiny. At the first Gaul port Cassian went ashore, and with a substantial amount of coin marched purposefully to meet with the village leaders. It seemed to take a lifetime, and finally when Spartacus declared he was going to find his friend and began to put his armour on, the recognisable figure that was Cassian came into view. It sauntered down the harbour a little unsteady upon his feet, at his side, a man tried his best to keep the Roman upright. After some rather undignified attempts to climb aboard finally Cassian planted his wavering torso upon the deck.

'The discussions went well?' Spartacus asked shaking his head in the process.

'Indeed very well, it would have dishonoured my hosts if I had refused to drink with them,' replied Cassian.

'Looks to me, like you honoured them a little too much.'

'No matter,' replied Cassian. Unable to remove the huge smile upon his face, 'i would like you to meet Vectrix. He will guide us to our destination and also put us in touch with a local leader who can help us there.'

'How do we know we can trust this man?' Plinius asked.

'I speak your language and so you can direct your questions to me, as for trust I don't see that you have much choice,' Vectrix spoke with supreme confidence, not shaken at being aboard a foreign vessel and surrounded by armed men.

'I meant no disrespect, but this journey has already taught us that we must be careful.'

'We should always be careful young man, but I am too old to involved in deceit and intrigue, I get paid to perform a task and I do it, nothing more, nothing less.'

'Then maybe you should tell us how long this journey will take,' interrupted Spartacus.

'That depends on whether or not the Gods allow us safe passage, now may I suggest that this Roman,' he gestured towards Cassian 'goes and takes a rest, the Roman legions maybe the envy of the known world, but their citizens have the drinking capacity of a small child.'

With Cassian safely resting below deck, the sailors erupted into movement. The flotilla moved on, the coast never too far from view. The nerves of the men becoming palpable now that they knew that within days they could be setting foot on the mysterious land believed to be home of all manner of magical creatures. Vectrix had heard some of the men talking, and laughed at their suggestions, claiming that he had traded upon those shores many times. The crew asked of the beasts that could devour men, and Vectrix claimed that in all his time he had not seen any strange beasts but when asked of the warriors that was a different matter. He talked in wonder at their aggression and indeed skill at warfare and also their tendency to keep the head of a fallen enemy. Spartacus was eager to learn more but waited for the crew to become quiet and for Vectrix to be alone.

'May I speak with you Vectrix?' he kept his voice low.

'Of course Spartacus,' replied Vectrix.

'You know who I am?'

'I do, we have actually met before. When your rebellion was at its height you traded for weapons up and down the coast, my brother had some profitable dealings with you.'

'Where is your brother now?'

'Last summer his vessel was taken by pirates, by good fortune I was making deals at the port of Tarraco, hence the reason I now find myself selling my skills. Let's hope this friend Cassian of yours, stays alive long enough to pay his debt to me.'

'Are you a betting man Vectrix?'

'Aren't we all Spartacus?'

'Then you have never placed a wager with more certain odds, backing Cassian will result in an excellent return.'

'But it's still a wager, and not a guarantee.'

'In life Vectrix, as you well know, nothing is certain. Now tell me more about these warriors, their strengths and weaknesses.'

The conversation lasted some time, Vectrix told of how the warriors fought for personal glory but still possessed a loyalty to their tribe to match any warriors he had met upon his wide travels. He talked of the women who held a magnificent beauty but could wield a sword as well as any man, how they painted themselves and often ran naked into battle. They did not fight in formation which was, he supposed a weakness, for they sort out individuals if possible. A battle was more a chance to settle old scores between individuals, the loser often ending his days as a head without a torso displayed within the enemies camp. He talked of their culture which was far more advanced than Spartacus had expected, when he was told of the beautiful jewellery they crafted and how they sang haunting melodies which spoke of loved ones lost.

'You seem to have a great deal of respect for these people?'

'They are a people of great honour, who are plain speaking and expect the same in return. They fight as if possessed by the Gods themselves, but can be gentile like a new born baby, and when one day the Romans decide to take that land as they will my own, they will find a people who will fight and when they are beaten as we all shall be, they will spit in the eye of the emperor.'

'I'm starting to like these people already and I am yet to meet one.'

'One moment,' as he spoke Vectrix jumped to his feet, and with a shout and a wave of the arms, the vessels changed direction and for the first time the little flotilla of boats headed out into open water.

All aboard knew this was the final stage of the journey to be made upon water. Many who had craved the stability of land, now wished to remain safely aboard the vessels. Spartacus however was in a more reflective mood, smiling to himself he recounted the trials of his life. Since reaching adulthood he had been fighting to stay alive, there was always those that must be defeated or loved ones that required saving. Many times he had wondered if it would ever end, whether or not he would be granted time to rest. If that rest would be in this world, or indeed the next he did not know. It seemed to him that the Gods played with his life as a small child plays with a toy, and they never tired of demanding sacrifice from him. Though his thoughts were grim, the smile never left him. Spartacus had somehow grown used to the tasks the Gods had forced upon him, he faced them now with an almost amused resignation.

Chapter XXII

The mood of the men seemed different, they busied themselves hardly raising their eyes from the tasks they had chosen to complete. As the coastline they had followed for so long fell further away, then so their mood became darker, each of them craving isolation. Behind them clear visibility to a vista they had become accustomed to like an old friend, they yearned for its safety. To the front a dense blanket of fog hid the dangers that awaited ready to strike from the gloom, even the most hardened warriors refused to look into the mists, as if the action would bring their thoughts of rampaging monsters to reality. The vessels ploughed on, and soon the mists engulfed each of them, the men were left no option but to take notice as each of the boats around them disappeared from view. Upon each vessel a lookout would call out, allowing the others belonging to the flotilla to know they were not alone. Cassian and Spartacus eyed the ominous mists, though both were known for being steady and unflinching before dangers, even those two wore a mask of anxiety. Aboard the entire fleet only one man seemed unconcerned by the spectral plain in which they found themselves. Vectrix smiled with amusement at the palpable tension which gripped the men, Spartacus couldn't help wondering whether he was an agent of Flabinus, sent to bring them all to ruin. The man smiled at him,

'Don't worry yourself, we will be through this shortly and land isn't far away.'

'How do you know? I cannot see a bloody thing,' replied Spartacus.

'I have travelled this way many time's, this is not an unusual sight in these parts. Trust me, you will see.'

Spartacus doubted his words, the mists were so dense he felt they would last forever, masking the flotilla from safety for the rest of time. He glanced behind and could see no more than a few paces from the stern of the boat, cursing, he knew that even the option of retreating the way they came was an impossibility. For by the time they had turned the vessels around, all bearings would be lost and they would sail on until starvation or madness took the men.

The suddenness in which the mists disappeared was almost as shocking as sailing through them, one moment near blindness and then the bright light of the day. Men screwed up their eyes until they adjusted to the change, and slowly they became aware of the land which lay before them. A number of cliffs rose from the murky waters like angry giants, ready to smash all that passed close by. However Vectrix told the crew to keep going, ignoring the rocks and the imposing cliffs. Vectrix simply moved his hands in the direction he wanted the flotilla to change its direction, it replied as an obedient steed eager to please its master. Amazingly the rocks began to become more and more sparse and then a gap appeared in the treacherous cliffs, suddenly sitting neatly, arms outstretched, welcoming the nervous vessels, a large cove. The relief could be heard as hardened men some of whom had fought on the battlefields of the known world not flinching in their task of kill or be killed, blew out their cheeks thanking the Gods for safe deliverance.

The surf caressed about the ankles of Cassian, he enjoyed the cold refreshing feeling as it washed over him, because no matter how wet the waves were, he revelled in the fact he could feel the sand beneath, cradling his feet. He tried hard not to show how much he enjoyed the experience, he eyed Vectrix who had found the journey rather too amusing. This causing Cassian to begin to get annoyed, his scout's over confidence prickling his nerves. They trudged their way up to ground which was firmer to the foot, Cassian stood up straight looking for any signs of civilisation.

'You have no need to look for them, they will find us. Indeed I will be surprised if they haven't already.'

'And just who are, they?'

'This land belongs to the Dumnonii, an interesting tribe to say the least.'

'In what way?' Cassian asked, 'do I have reason to be worried?'

'Though I do not claim to know all of these lands, I do claim that I have travelled the coastal regions quite extensively. I have encountered many of the tribes, but the Dumnonii stand out from the rest in so many ways.'

'Militarily?'

'Oh they have some fine warriors but many of the tribes do so, the difference is in how they have developed socially compared to their neighbours. They have no king or any ruling classes, not which that I can discern. No major city where the powerful dwell and dictate orders for the rest of the kingdom, and yet despite all this they remain a closely bonded people though many live in small villages they seem to think as one.'

'Surely that makes them easy prey for neighbouring tribes.'

'Well they do not use coin, so they have no evident wealth and they also have warriors that possess great skill. Put those two together and I suppose an enemy must think long and hard whether invading such a place is worth the loss of men on their own side. Besides the fact they have no king, they seemed to have gained a great reputation for politics and have married a number of their women to influential families, into the royal households of many of their neighbour tribes.'

'It is ingenious how people find ways to survive, so when do we meet this tribe?'

'I am surprised we have not met them already, this part of the coast is usually watched constantly by members of this tribe, any traders usually come this way. We will have to travel to one of the smaller villages, it lies just over those hills,' Vectrix pointed as he spoke.

'We cannot leave the vessels out to sea, we do not know how long this will take. I will call the men in and have them make camp and a number of us will endeavour to find this village of which you talk.'

'Always cautious, Cassian?'

'Careless men in my trade Vectrix usually run out of breathe quickly,' Cassian strode away from his guide and signalled to the rest of the men to come ashore.'

'I would have thought I had proven I was trustworthy by bringing you through the mists.'

'Then you are wrong, the man we hunt is cruel and vindictive but most of all he is intelligent. Other men seem to wish to worship him, as if he was a God that walks among us. They therefore will do any bidding that he demands, no matter how despicable. So forgive me I do not wish to slight your pride but I trust few men, most of which are on those vessels you see in front of you.' Vectrix did not reply, merely watched his employer walk away.

It took time for the other men to come ashore, only a handful of men were left aboard the boats. Camp was made upon the beach, sentries were set and armour donned for this was a foreign land and they had only Vectrix' word that the natives were unlikely to attack. When the men had made order from the landing, Cassian selected a number of men who would scout with himself in search

275

of the village. He asked Spartacus to stay behind to ensure the camp was well guarded, but he took Plinius and Tictus and a number of Orin's riders. They had not brought many horses with them, so altogether the scouting party numbered thirteen, they travelled fast promising Spartacus they would at least send word of their progress by nightfall. As it were, it had only just passed midday when the leading horsemen called out that they could see smoke in the distance. It was not long before they spotted people heading towards them down the muddy track. Women and children, cuts and bruises evident upon their features, the true extent of which hidden by the black soot which covered each of them. Vectrix pushed his horse forward keen to know more, the anguish shown on his features shocked Cassian, the man had seemed oblivious to anyone's woes to that point. Cassian ordered the rest of the men to dismount and give aid where they could. He watched the old Gaul move from villager to villager trying to piece together what had happened. The language was similar to what Vectrix spoke and Cassian recognised some of the words, but piecing together what had taken place from such fragments was all but impossible.

'Tictus, Plinius here quickly,' Cassian called. The two men moved instantly to his side ready to do his bidding. 'From what I can gather to our front there is a village, I want you to scout it and find out what has happened. Listen to me do not engage any of the enemy, for a start we do not know who has done this. I will send for the rest of the men but it will take time, myself and Vectrix will stay here and tend to these people they have walked enough for one day.' Tictus and Plinius nodded their compliance and raced off towards the smoke that now dominated the horizon.

'Thank you Cassian,' whispered Vectrix.

'We need to make these people comfortable, I fear for the rest of the village.'

'You have done all that you could, these people know that.'

Plinius and Tictus did not get too close before they dismounted and skirted around the village searching for the perfect position to observe the surrounding area. At first an eerie calm had seemed to have settled over the village, the fires that had once raged had now shrunk back and merely threw a thick black cloud into the sky. If it had been an army that had attacked this village, then they no longer appeared to be in residence. Bodies littered the ground, Tictus fought back the urge to vomit. The thought of doing so in front of Plinius would fill him with shame, so he tried with all his will to focus on the task of scouting the horizon looking for enemy. Plinius seemed to know what troubled his friend,

'The first time I saw something like this, I retched so bad I thought my arse would come through my mouth.'

'Does it get any better?'

'The sad thing is Tictus, is that you harden yourself to such sights. I am not sure a man should ever do so, for the horror should live in all of us. That way we will be certain never let the beast within take control, and deliver similar fates to other poor souls.' A scream rent the air, Tictus went to rise but Plinius held him firm,

'Do not race to a fight, until you know you can win it. Or at least have a fighting chance.'

Before them a family emerged from behind a hut, they had obviously hidden when the enemy had come, but the attackers had expected as much and not all had left with the army. One man stood before those attackers, he already bled from both side and thigh, behind him a female and three children. The attackers laughed, the numbers clearly giving them great confidence. Though Plinius noticed, that not one of the seven attackers was too keen on being the first to test the man's blade, which dripped with

278

blood. Obviously the lone defender had already, proven he was no easy kill to these murderers. Plinius watched the man, he moved with some skill not allowing his enemy to out flank him and doing his best to protect those to his rear.

'Listen to me Tictus, do exactly as I say. Skirt around the buildings and find a good vantage point to use your bow. Be quick now we don't have much time.'

'What are you going to do?'

'Me?' Plinius laughed. 'I'm going to pick a fight.'

The assailants had just about plucked up enough courage to try and charge the defiant villager, when a cough from behind them, stopped all in their tracks. The largest of the group yelled in some strange language, which Plinius could only assume meant, that he was not welcome. He held his ground and smiled at the man, the warrior before him raised up the massive sword he held, and shook it menacingly at the smiling young man before him. Anger flushed upon the man's face, he charged in a blind fury. That fury never stopped until a blade ripped out both of his knees caps, he had not even see the young man move. Now he lay on the ground, his blood mixing with the dark mud which seemed to be common place within these lands. Plinius took a step to the front and with one blow sent the injured man to the next world. A second warrior moved towards Plinius intent on avenging the death of his comrade but he had learnt enough to be wary. But his caution did him not good as a shaft burst into his neck, he slumped harmlessly to the ground, only the gurgle of breathe on blood could be heard as the man fought to fill his lungs. Another shaft took an attacker in the thigh, he yelped with pain and before long he was running the best he could from the village. The others lost heart too, no soldier likes to fight an enemy they cannot see and the whereabouts of the archer was a mystery to them. Plinius tried for some time to explain who he was to the villager, but eventually gave up simply calling Vectrix' name in the hope the man knew their guide. It worked and slowly uneasily the villagers followed Tictus and Plinius back along the muddy track to find Cassian. Though the adult villagers were at first wary of Plinius and Tictus, eventually they began to relax. The large warrior trying his best to communicate with the two strangers, who had come to his family's rescue. It was an awkward affair with both parties becoming frustrated at the lack of understanding on both sides. Soon the attempts stalled and then stopped and they concentrated upon their journey. One of the children approached Plinius, the first that

Plinius was aware of this fact was when the young boy slipped his hand inside his. Plinius looked down at the child, initially the warrior was startled but managed a smile. The boy squeezed his hand tightly as he beamed a smile, Plinius bent and lifted him, pretending to pinch the boy's nose. The child laughed, his whole body trembling as he did so. The infectious tremor caused Plinius to erupt with laughter, and he held the boy close and ruffled his hair.

Cassian had been watching the track for his scouts, he could not help be amazed by the sight. His two scouts and a number of villagers came towards him, but upon the shoulders of Plinius there was a child and another walked at his side holding his hand. He strode out to meet this strange apparition,

'Been making friends Plinius?'

'I am sorry Cassian, we had to intervene.'

Cassian looked from his men to the villagers, especially at the injuries upon the male. Then finally he looked into the eyes of the children, he bent a stroked the cheek of the child nearest to him.

'Plinius I trust your judgement if you say it was necessary to intervene, then it was necessary. Now let's make these people more comfortable and then you can give me a more detailed report.'

Chapter XXIII

The following morning, Cassian and his men accompanied Vectrix and the villagers back to their homes. The bodies were burned and riders sent to neighbouring villages, before the sun had fully risen in the sky, help arrived from all over the tribe's lands. Cassian however, while all the men were busy repairing homes and tending the wounded, pulled Vectrix to one side. He needed to know what he and his men had walked into, whether this was some kind of sporadic raid which was normal in these parts or the beginnings of a war.

'You do not understand Cassian, these people have no enemies. They are a simple people, as I have said before they have no real wealth to speak of. Their neighbours respect their ways, and all rely upon the trade in which they have developed with one another.'

'There is no tribe that would want these lands,' Cassian asked. Vectrix looked thoughtful and as though struck by a lightning bolt replied. 'These lands no but the lands to the east belonging to the tribe Durotriges, they have become rich from trade with Gaul.'

'You think they are responsible for this?'

'No, they have excellent relations with the Dumnonii, however a tribe to the north have been making moves on lands which belong to their allies, I am sure the wealth of the Durotriges is the real ambition. Maybe they believe if they can eradicate the allies one by one then the Durotriges will be a far easier kill come the end.'

'Who is this tribe and where do they originate?'

'It is a truly savage tribe which lies to the far north, a mountain people known as the Ordovices, little is known about them. All I can testify to the character of such individuals of that tribe, are the slaughtered remains of fellow traders I have come across. But this is most unlike them, subterfuge is not what they are known for.'

'But the man I seek in these lands is filled with deceit, he would see these people as an opportunit…..,' Cassian broke off as his eye was caught by movement behind Vectrix.

Vectrix turned to observe an army, it must have been at least four thousand strong and it appeared from the trees like spectres. Cassian's hand instinctively moved towards his blade but the old scout stayed his arm,

'These are the warriors of Dumnonii, it would not bode well for you to show aggression.'

'Then speak to them Vectrix, tell them that we have only offered friendship and help to their people.' However, as Vectorix made to walk towards the spectral army shouts came from the eastern side of the village and slowly as all turned to look in the direction of the shouts, upon the hillside to the east another army appeared at least twice the size of the initial one.

'By the Gods,' cursed Vectrix.

'Who are they?' Cassian asked, seeing the panic upon the Gaul's face.

'Durotriges, but I don't understand.'

But Cassian did, it was an old Roman trick. Before you invade a land you make your enemies weaken each other. A burned village here, a poisoned member of royalty there, with just enough evidence so each side blamed one another. Then when one weakened victor stands alone, you move in and take all that you want, and Flabinus was the master of such ploys, Cassian knew this was his work and inwardly promised to end it before it began.

'Vectrix! Go speak to the Durotriges and send someone you trust to speak to their own people let them know we are here to help.'

The scout did as he was told and for what seemed like an age, Cassian and his men stood between two sets of mighty warriors and if the talks went badly, he and his men stood no chance of holding back the tide of violence, which would wash over them. Most of Cassian's men could not help continually glancing from one imposing army to another. Only Spartacus remained calm, he portrayed a man who simply idled in the sun. He sat down and whistled a tune, and paid the hordes of warriors no heed, Plinius guessed this was for the men's benefit, but was still amazed at Spartacus' coolness in face of overwhelming odds.

At last Vectrix and a number of what Cassian could only guess were military leaders made their way down the hillside. They stopped short of entering the village and waited for their counter parts from the Dumnonii army to leave the trees. As the two sets of leaders met on the outskirts of the village and then moved to the centre and occupying an elongated hut that dominated the nearby surroundings. Cassian and his men again found themselves playing the waiting game, Cassian thought to himself that the leaders of these tribes had taken a massive risk entering the village with only a small bodyguard. If they expect men to act with respect and honour then they will truly fall prey to men like Flabinus, and though he hated to admit it, to men even like himself, or at least how he had once been. The day was wearing on, and the sun had already started its slow descent beneath the distant hills, when Vectrix finally emerged from the doorway of the hut.

'Cassian, you are required within.' With the ending of his words he simply turned and disappeared, making it clear to Cassian that the request was in fact an order. Once inside he found the leaders seated upon the floor, wine had been drank readily and to his surprise, he was offered a goblet. Rather more surprising was the ornate metal work which had been carried out upon the goblet, it reminded him of the words his father used to use,

'If you wish to judge how truly civilised a nation is Cassian, then do not look at the weapons their army's carry, or the wealth they hold in their vaults. Merely look upon their works of art, for art comes from the heart and cannot be earned from the point of a sword.'

As strange as it seemed, Cassian had never really knew what he meant until this moment. The goblet was indeed beautiful, and although all else seemed basic, these people clearly thought far more deeply than the average Roman citizen would ever believe them possible. Such craftsmanship was not learnt in a moment, this craft took a lifetime to master and must be passed from generation to generation, and so already Cassian was beginning to reassess his hosts, and indeed the father he had struggled to understand for many years.

'Cassian, these men are held in high esteem by the members of their tribes. They are both learned in the way of the sword and of the world. You will answer them honestly, prey do not try to deceive them, both sets have lost friend and family this day and are running short on forgiveness.'

'I prize my honour, as high as their prize theirs Vectrix.' Cassian puffed out his chest as he spoke, he would not be treated as a little boy at a adults meeting. Before Vectrix could reply one of the Dumnonii warriors began to laugh.

'You crow loud Roman, I like that. I am Penduim,' as he spoke he held out his arm for Cassian to take. 'i have seen and heard of what you did for my people in this village. For that I call you friend, and owe you a great debt.'

Shocked that the warrior could speak his language made Cassian hesitate but regaining himself replied 'I am honoured Penduim, but you owe me no debt, I believe the man responsible for the attack on this village was once of my tribe, I hunt the man for carrying out similar actions against my own people.'

'This man has been spotted with a war band of Ordovice, they move quickly to the north with captives and plunder. But to follow them would do no good, they head for the wolf's head, a heavily fortified encampment which cannot be breached.'

'Why?'

'It is a fearsome place, stockade after stockade prevent, any attack. Before the stockade a huge ditch with sharpened rocks, they jut from the ground like teeth, ready to tear at the flesh of any unfortunate soul.'

'If the stockades were swept away, would you be willing to help me and my men take that place and kill those that have wronged us.'

'Would it be so, but I fear with your men and mine we will still come up short.' Both turned at the same time to look at the Durotrige leaders, who at first looked back in confusion and then a large smile appeared on his face, apparently words of war transcended all languages.

Two days had passed and the preparations had gone well, Penduim had provided Cassian with a much more detailed plan of the wolf's head. Cassian had up to this point refused to tell him how he intended to sweep away the formidable defences that they would face. Until three large wagons rolled into the village centre, the wagons straining under their substantial loads. Cassian had sent for them almost immediately and it had taken all this time to carry their cargo from his vessels.

'Penduim you know I told you that I would cast aside the enemy's stockades.'

'I cannot see it being possible.'

'I have a powerful friend, who despite being the governor of a wealthy city, always finds time to play with his little toys. These toys he gave me as a gift, for these men you see around you carried out a great service for him and he wishes the destruction of Flabinus as much as any man. What these wagons hold will sweep those defences aside, like the blade takes down long grass, giving us the opportunity to storm the stronghold.'

'I prey you are correct, for to me they look like a pile of lumber.'

'The area this fortress is situated, will I be able to get these weapons to approach the walls?'

'Yes, the front approach is a flat plain and only the teeth of the wolf, guard the run up to the fortifications.'

'Then you have my word, the stockade walls will be swept away and any of the defending warriors that stay at their post will be taken with them.'

Penduim smiled at Cassian's words, though inwardly he still wondered how this strange Roman believed the wagon's contents could remove the walls that had stood many an attack. While Cassian made his plans, Spartacus gave the men more instruction in the art of war, many of the tribal warriors watched with amusement. They cared not for the way these strange men from across the water seemed to work in unison, where was the individual glory in such battle. Spartacus eventually got annoyed at one such warrior who continually hurled insults at the men, laughing with derision. Not wanting to upset the alliance forged by Cassian, he asked Vectrix to arrange a playful contest between himself and the warrior to boost the morale of the troops who would soon go to war. The Durotrige warriors got a little annoyed that they were not asked to submit a warrior and Spartacus soon agreed that a third fighter would enter the contest.

'You know Spartacus, you are not a young man any more perhaps I should take your place,' Plinius laughed.

'Plinius I have taught you all that you know, but that is just a fraction of what I know. Let's hope you live long enough to challenge me in the arena.' The rebuff landed a little harder than it was meant to, and Spartacus saw its impact for it made Plinius redden in the face. 'but in front of all the men here and the Gods themselves I swear there is no man I would rather have at my side when entering battle.'

Instantly Plinius cheered, having the admiration of Spartacus meant more to him than all the gold he had won in the arena of Utica. The cheers rose as the three warriors moved into battle, wooden swords at the ready. Though it was unlikely a severe injury would be inflicted, the weapons still caused a great deal of pain especially when wielded by such powerful warriors. The sun went down to the cheers of warriors, to the north stood an arrogant man pleased with the tasks he had completed so far in these lands. He afforded himself a little chuckle, these people were like lambs they moved to his slightest command and died when they must. He had seen the various tribes of this land, and though strong and brave they lacked the intelligence to realise their potential. Those that did not strive to improve will always be victim to those that do. The ambitious would become rich while the brave and strong fed the carrion birds or learned to bow their heads. At that moment his thoughts were interrupted, as the Ordovice chieftain moved to his shoulder,

'What now Flabinus, do we prepare for war.?'

'You left evidence which would link the raids to other tribes?'

'It was done,' replied the chief. He barely disguised the disgust he felt for the man before him, but he would bring power to the Ordovice and therefore must be tolerated.

'Then we wait for our enemies to tear themselves apart, and those that remain standing will be far too weak to resist us, but I am sure their will plenty of trophies for you and your men win.'

Chapter XXIV

Blades were honed to enable the maximum destruction, armour polished and men fed well. The time had come Spartacus had set foot on this land less than five days ago and he found himself going to war once again. He would kill or be killed by men with whom he had never even had an argument; he shook his head as he tied the straps which held his breastplate in place. Arthurax who had hardly left the side of Spartacus since being well and truly beaten in the contest, gone was the scorn he poured onto to the foreigners for the way they fought. Replaced with a reverence for the skill that Spartacus had shown that day, the cuts and bruises he had suffered still made him wince with pain from time to time. The agony of which only made him more aware of the power and skill of the muscled warrior next to him. Spartacus held no malice towards the man and they even took the time to learn a little of each other's language. Spartacus watched Cassian giving some last minute instruction to some scouts, the language obstacle overcome with the help from Penduim. Then suddenly the call went up and thousands of warriors rose as one, there was no cheer, merely a resignation to a task that must be done. Thousands of men moved in unison towards the north to do battle with a tribe that had struck fear into the hearts of the people of these lands for decades. Their enemy so often appearing from the dark, to kill and slaughter without mercy. Now they would seek the beast in its lair the fabled Wolf's head a fortress as yet to be breached by mere mortals. As Spartacus looked around the men he observed the uncertainty in their eyes, whatever plan Cassian had, best work for these men were not the trained organised legions of Rome. Discipline came as second nature to those soldiers, but how these tribesmen would react to a battle where they must take the exacting toll of missile fire long before they came to grips with the enemy he did not know. He had seen many a brave man turn and run in such circumstances driven to despair by the maelstrom of missiles. He knew his men would stand, he knew the enemy would fight for they had no choice but as for his allies, only the Gods knew whether they would run or bravely stand at his side.

The rains came, turning the tracks into mud baths which sucked at feet and even worse the heavily laden wagons. The freshly polished armour soon turned to a deep brown mess as each soldier struggle to move the wagons forward. The only benefit to the rains was that they made the march so difficult many of the men did not have time to dwell on the upcoming engagement. By the end of the first day the men were already exhausted, thick mud coated almost every inch of their bodies, it clung to them weighing each man down. The rain still continued to pour down upon them as they tried to find cover and enable the exhausted to sleep. Men shrank away from the downfall, often clinging to the trunk of a tree, anything that would keep the water away from their already soaked bodies. Eventually no matter how wet or uncomfortable their place to rest, all fell to slumber the tiredness taking them. Cassian watched the army and wondered how such general as Alexander had faced conditions like these continuously and still managed wondrous victory after victory. Spartacus slumped down next to him, the warrior had spent time with the guards ensuring they would not fall asleep.

'An interesting day to say the least Cassian.'

'I am no military man Spartacus, am I leading these poor souls on a fool's errand?'

'You are doing just fine, no matter the greatness of the leader they cannot control the weather.'

'The Gods can, have I displeased them in some way?'

'Quiet that talk, you know I have no time for the Gods, for they have had little or no time for me. But some in your ranks will hold great store by what they think the Gods intend, do not even whisper that the eternal beings are displeased, nothing will make this army disband quicker.'

'I am sorry but look at them,' Cassian shook his head, 'how will they fight at the end of such a journey?'

'They are wet and dirty, that's soldiering Cassian. Come the morning and hopefully the sun, this day will be forgotten.'

'I hope you are right Spartacus, more days of this will sap the strength from the men.'

'That's the Cassian we all know, morbid as ever. Get some sleep it will be better in the morning. Besides no point in worrying about disaster, It's never too far away.'

'Thank you Spartacus, that makes me feel a whole lot better.' Spartacus laughed, and settled down after first lying his cloak on the ground. It did not take long before the damp soaked through the thick cloth, but the tiredness had overwhelmed him and soon he slept.

The following day Cassian looked at Spartacus in awe, as though the warrior was some profit of the Gods, for the sun shone brilliantly down upon them. So much so, that many of the men had to hold their hands to their eyes, to prevent the glare impairing their sight. The slow sombre movement that had accompanied the movements of the men, had evaporated with the damp that they had been forced to lay upon. As they ate their morning meal, the smiles began to return with even a little laughter returning to the camp. Penduim approached Cassian and Spartacus,

'The Durotriges are moving out.'

'What! They are leaving?' a shocked Spartacus replied.

'Calm yourself Spartacus,' spoke Cassian 'it is all part of the plan.'

'You become worried Spartacus, afraid we cannot take the fortress ourselves,' Penduim jested.

'To get to that bastard Flabinus I would take the place by myself......though in truth I would rather not have to,' he quickly added.

'My people will fight Spartacus, you need not fear in this matter.'

'And what about them?' Spartacus asked pointing in the direction of the Durotriges.

'They are an honourable race with fine warriors, but nothing is certain war.'

Spartacus did not speak further but stared ruefully in the direction they must journey to complete the task before them. He knew splitting the army was common practice while marching, however it also made an army vulnerable to attack. Preventing it from concentrating its full force and easy prey if a intelligent enemy was nearby.

As it was, the ranks of men marching with Spartacus began to swell. For as they passed through lands of other tribes, they too joined the fight against a common enemy. Many of them had suffered years of raids upon villages, which had left so many dead and without homes. The rains never returned, and so with the extra men and the small tracks drying out, traversing the landscape with the heavy wagons became easier. They were making good time, Spartacus began to worry that they would be seen by Ordovice scouts,

'It is not unusual, you have to understand Spartacus that we had been plagued by these people for longer than I can remember. Our people have rose up against them before, and when they smash against that cursed fortress, they are slaughtered without getting close enough to spit on the Ordovice. They do not fear attack, all they have to do is stay within that gruesome place and we are powerless.'

'We had a name for men without fear in the gladiator ludus.'

'What was that?'

'The dead.'

Penduim laughed, 'I hope you are right, this tribe has blighted these lands for long enough, my own father fell to one of their spears. That is a debt well over due, one which I plan to collect on very shortly.'

The conversation was halted by scouts racing towards Cassian and Penduim, after a short conversation, it was clear the fortress had been spotted.

'Penduim may I suggest you send your best men to watch for any enemy, tonight we camp here. The men will need to rest and we need to give the Durotriges time to get into position.'

'Where are they?' Spartacus asked.

'They have circled around the fortress, we do not need anyone slipping past our men in the chaos of battle.'

Spartacus knew to whom Cassian referred, it was unlikely that Flabinus would like being trapped with nowhere to run and if there was a passage to safety, then he would take it. There would be no fires that night, cold meat and wine were consumed but not one man drank too much, the next day would bring a great battle and the clearer the head the more chance to see another morning. The men settled down, in truth they did not sleep much, but the camp was quiet with just slight movement when the change of guard took place. As the men battled the spectres of fear that ravaged all men before war, Cassian and Spartacus silently left camp to take their first look at the mighty fortress. To the people of these lands it was formidable but for a former soldier and gladiator of Rome like Spartacus, it held no such fear. Yes men would die taking it, but if the weaponry that Cassian had brought with him did what it was designed to do, then many of the defences would be swept away. That left the ditch, which Penduim had told them was filled with thousands of sharpened rocks. Spartacus had been surprised by this as sharpened wooden stakes would have been far better for the task. It seemed the Ordovice liked to build upon the legend of the Wolf's Head, feeling that jagged rocks far more resembled teeth than wooden stakes. Cassian had fallen silent, Spartacus moved closer to him and whispered,

'We do not know, if Flabinus is even in this place.'

301

'Oh he is there Spartacus, I can feel the bastard.'

'You realise that you cannot enter the battle, you will be needed to direct the movement of your men. For I cannot oversee the engagement, I do not yet know enough of the language and besides you have gained their trust.'

'I know Spartacus, it is enough that the man dies. But if possible I would like to be present when it happens, so when you find him. Try not to kill him too quickly, but take no risks.'

'If it is within my power you will witness his final breath, you have my word.'

The two men strode slowly back to camp the sun already beginning to rise, surprisingly many of the men were already awake,

'You see Cassian, they have reached the bridge.'

'What bridge, what do you mean?' confusion upon his face.

'When men know that a battle is coming, a spectral road spreads before them. As they journey along it, they glance from side to side hoping to see another route. Sometimes they will glance back and see loved ones waving to them or an action that they have taken. But eventually they will reach the bridge and they know the only way to go, is to cross, that is when a man is ready

302

for battle. When they just want it out of the way, so they can continue upon their journey.'

'And are you ready to cross the bridge Spartacus?'

'I seem to have spent my bloody life on the bridge, maybe this will be the last battle and I will be allowed to continue my journey.'

'We can but hope the Gods see fit to allow it, though I don't hope too much.' Cassian smiled. Penduim approached a smile broad upon his face,

'I have news, the Durotriges are in place. Not only that, they are as yet undetected lying in the trees just to the north of the fortress.'

'Excellent, get all the men ready to move. Send word to our allies to ensure they are prepared and in place, lets close this trap and see what our enemy will do.'

Cassian finished his final orders and then watched the fortress before him. He wondered how many traps lay hidden, waiting to snare and drag his men to oblivion. He hoped that those that prepared the fortification were as lazy has those that set the scouts. Glancing to the skies, he silently gave a short prayer. He rarely paid homage to the God's, preferring to trust in men but at this time, in this place he would take all the good fortune he could, and from any quarter.

Chapter XXV

Flabinus belched the belch of a contented man, he rubbed his stomach. He was not the type of man, who usually indulged in too much in gluttony, and has he stared down at his plate, he made a vow to complete a vigorous day of training. For as much as Flabinus was a vicious killer, he was also extremely vain, and doted upon his own reflection. He traced the scar upon his face with his finger and cursed warrior responsible. It was then that one of his own men, burst into his quarters,

'Flabinus come quick, we have a problem.'

Flabinus would have scolded the man, but no sooner had he made his announcement than he had darted back from the room. A feeling stirred within Flabinus, usually men feared him more than any issue that might arise but his own man had not waited to be dismissed. It was not pleasant, a man like himself relied heavily upon the fear they instilled within all they met. He wanted to run from the room and see for himself exactly what had generated such fear, but instead he stood calmly, straightened his tunic, wiping any debris food from the front. Then he walked serenely from his quarters as though he was just about to take the morning air before bathing, not a trouble in the world. Looking around he saw the tribesmen and his own men on the stockade, all were pointing and talking hurriedly. He took his time wishing to show all that dwelled there, that he did not fluster easily. He climbed the ladder, now wishing he had enjoyed a lighter meal. He joined his men at the top of the highest rampart, and followed their gaze beyond the perimeter of the fortress. His training allowed his body to remain calm, but if his men had seen his eyes they would have seen shock with just a trace of despair.

Cassian's army of mixed tribes, and his own men did indeed look impressive. The trap had closed beautifully, the enemy unaware of any danger until the very last moment. A small group of men including Cassian and Spartacus began to draw up the battle orders. The selected few closed in about him to hear what tasks they must do.

'Boucca and Garlanni, your men will hold the perimeter and will not take part in the main assault,' Cassian wanted to rush over this part fearing the Durotrige leaders would take offense at not being given the chance for glory 'but your role is probably the most important within the battle plan, it will be your duty to

306

prevent the Ordovice reinforcing from your side of the fortress. Keep making sporadic attacks along the defences to keep the enemy guessing and tied down.' Cassian stopped to allow Vectrix the chance to translate, he hoped that the translation was not missing any important detail. It would be all too easy for the plan to go wrong. 'It is important that you do not enter into a full scale attack until my troop and the Dumnonii have cleared the first line of defences, your men will be facing undamaged fortifications and would rather you not throw men away needlessly. Again he paused to allow Vectrix to once again convey his message.

He watched their response closely. As Vectrix finished his words the Durotrige faces showed their comprehension of the plan, and they beamed large snarling smiles. They nodded in approval of the plan and then held their weapons aloft and let out some kind of war cry which was lost on Cassian and Spartacus but was answered in kind by Penduim. Clearly not interested in any other players role within the battle they turned and left to join their men.

'Penduim once the catapult have broken the enemy's defences my men will lead the first attack, their armour and larger shields will afford them some protection against the missile fire they will face. I want you to organise you men into four lines of attack, each

307

line of attack will not advance until the previous one has cleared the ditch.'

'I understand men must have room to move within that place,' his face became dark as he spoke, clearly the ditch was the most feared part of this assault, 'if we slow down too much in there, we will be slaughtered like swine.'

'Exactly, the advance will not start until the first stockade has been cleared, and while the rank moves forward we will try and clear their secondary defences with the catapults.' As if his words had summoned the destructive beasts, the catapults were manoeuvred into position. 'Each wave of men will take ladders with then to help traverse the ditch, let us hope the Wolf's jaw is not snapping too much this day,' all nodding their agreement, 'Spartacus you may chose your own position upon the battlefield.'

'I will lead the first attack,' replied Spartacus.

'But…'

'Now don't start, these men will need to see a man they recognise to their front. You are needed here, I am an obvious choice.'

'Our friends will want to go with you, they will not allow you to go into that place alone.'

308

'Then let them come, they did not sign up for this mission for its safety. But best keep Aegis with you, this is a task that requires shield work. He will struggle to protect himself.'

'I will try to keep him busy, he won't like it one bit.' Cassian turned and faced the fortress which jutted from the ground before them, the sudden realisation that all the planning was done made he's hands tremble and sweat. For now he knew men must die, and it was upon his plans that the day depended.

Silence fell upon the battle field, the defenders eyed the horde which now faced them and the attackers were filled with anxiety. The fortress was almost legend amongst the tribes of this land and too many were letting those legendary stories play upon their minds.

'I think this is where you address the men Cassian.'

'I don't think I can,' whispered Cassian in reply.

'Well its time I earned my coin then, Vectrix with me.' Spartacus strode out and turned to face the men. He paced along the line making eye contact with has many as possible, letting them wait before he began to speak,

'Many of you do not know me, but today we face a common enemy and will fight side by side. This day we will meet the men

face to face who have taken our loved ones and our friends. We are brothers in loss, the blood of that loss has tied us together as one, in an unbreakable bond which will never be broken. We will take vengeance upon those that have wronged us, I will not let the beasts that have committed these crimes against my brothers walk free this day. Look to me, I will be at your front, I will storm that ditch and those walls and slaughter any beast that stands in my way, all I want to know is will you fight my brothers?'

Vectrix finished translating only moments later putting as much vigour into the words as he could, all along the ranks cheering erupted building to a resounding battle cry, the eyes which showed the anxiety previously chased away to be replaced by anger and determination. As finally, the war cry died down, Cassian nodded and three large wooden arms roared into action. The catapults answered the call for battle and sent their deadly load soaring into the air.

Three enormous boulders arched high into the sky and then came crashing to the ground, the first disappeared into the ditch, the second fell harmlessly on the plain but the third cleared the ditch hitting the ground fifty paces before the fortifications, bounced and then bounced again. It turned over and over until it finally came to rest at foot of the fortifications placing a gentle kiss upon the wooden structure as it came to a stop. The defenders rushed to look at the monstrous rock leaning out of the fortification to get a clear look of how close it came, then the defenders cheered and hurled derisive insults at the attackers. A huge banner waving Ordovice even took the time to bare his arse to the attackers, as if insulted the catapults fired again. The arse baring warrior turned just in time to see a huge shadow fall over him, his section of the defences exploded in timber splinters and bloody pulp, a red mist hanging over the tattered remains of the damaged fortifications for quite some time. This time it was the attackers who raised their cheers, all of them rejoicing at the fortress weakening before their very eyes. Time and time again the might weapons of war fired their deadly missiles towards their foe, over and over timbers smashed and men died. The defenders at first tried to hide from the destruction reluctant to leave the outer defences, but as more and more holes were punched through the wooden timbers and more and more of their kinsmen fell without being able to strike a blow in return. They started to filter away from their original positions. But even as they reached their secondary position the deadly catapults found their range once again. Spartacus looked to

Cassian, waiting for the signal to advance but Cassian shook his head, he knew he must order the advance at some point and dreaded when he must, but the very least he could for his friends and his men was create as much chaos in the enemies ranks as possible. The deadly fire continued until no missiles could be found to hurl at the enemy and at last Cassian looked to Spartacus and waved his men forward. Spartacus turned from his friend and now commander, raised his sword pointed towards the fortress and strode forward.

Plinius fell in alongside Spartacus, whereas Tictus, Melachus, Lathyrus and Orin spread themselves along the line, somehow believing that if they all bunched together one or more was bound to fall. Onward the first wave marched, Spartacus set a nice steady pace wanting the men as fresh as possible for the upcoming battle. He knew that to get over that ditch, up the slope and through the breach that had been created and then fight at the end of it, would test the men to exhaustion. He also kept the line tight, ensuring no gaps appeared, he needed these men to act as a single unit, shields the only barrier against the maelstrom of missiles which would surely come. Tictus raw when it came to war, did not look at the fortress but watched his own feet, blood pumped rapidly through

312

his veins, his heart beating so loudly that it dulled all other sounds. He felt the sword slipping against his sweating palm, he gripped even tighter making his knuckles shine white from the pressure. If any man had the time to watch the young warrior, they may have believed him too frightened to fight. That however was not concerned Tictus, yes he was scared to fall in battle, but his real fear was in letting down his friends. Failing at not being the man he hoped to be, he no longer wished to be the arrogant whelp his father had nurtured. So despite his fear one foot followed the next, in perfect order the line moved ever closer to the fortress.

Observing the advancing troops the defenders began to swarm back to the outer defences, they pulled their own dead out of the way, many slipping on blood and body parts of comrades already slain. The defenders collected whatever missiles they could, not only spears but whatever they could find to hand, a good sized rock could fell the enemy just as well as the spear tip. Spartacus neared the ditch, he ordered his men to close any gaps and the ladders to be brought forward, he knew that the enemy were waiting for his men to enter the ditch before launching their missile attack, where it would deliver the most damage. His throat was dry as he gave the order to advance, it was time for the men about him, to start to die.

'Are you with me Plinius?'

'To the very end Spartacus,' came the reply.

'Good then keep that bloody shield up, and no heroics. Do you understand? That's an order.'

'No fear on that.'

'Good man,' with that Spartacus momentarily turned his back to the enemy and faced his own men. 'Now, kill the bastards,' he roared.

Chapter XXVI

'Wine, Cassian?' Aegis asked.

'Yes please, I hope the Gods grant us the chance to share a drink with our friends when this is all over.'

Aegis did not answer he brooded over the fact that he was not fighting alongside those friends, he knew it made sense and he could yield a weapon, shield and traverse that ditch but it rankled with him that his friends risked all while he sipped wine and watched from safety. They watched Spartacus' men stop form up and then start to disappear into the ground, the exact location of the ditch lost from view. As they disappeared the defenders answered with missiles, the dark shapes emanating from the defences looked like a plague of locust rising into the air and then suddenly swooping down ominously onto Spartacus and his men.

Spartacus heard the screams and felt the missiles drumming against his shield, he gave the order and ladders were lowered into the pit, men died as they became exposed to the deadly hail. Screams and blood erupted as they worked their way into the deep ditch, designed for such slaughter. Some of his men were killed outright by missiles, others were thrown off balance and fell, they crashed down onto the sharpened rocks which impaled and smashed skulls and bone. Then Spartacus was picking his way across the ditch, no idea of how many men still followed him, the sheer volume of missiles ensuring his view consisted only of the back of his shield. Finally he reached the far side, at least the angle of the pit wall afforded him some respite from the murderous volleys from the defenders. Ladders smashed against the pit wall and at least for the time being, he still had men left alive, he glanced around making sure the men were ready to scale the ditch wall and once again enter the range of those defenders raining down their deadly fire. He roared encouragement to those around him, and began to climb the ladder, his shield held as best he could above him. Cassian waved the second line of infantry forward with Penduim barking out his commands.

Spartacus found himself free of the ditch, he straightened wondering if any others had made it to the summit, as he did shields locked in beside him and he breathed a sigh of relief. With the shield wall in place he chanced a look behind him, the ditch was strewn with bodies, and there approaching from the far side of the ditch came the first wave of Dumnonii. Penduim stood waving

316

his people on, the large warrior had discarded his shield and almost defied the defenders to dare shoot at him. Spartacus called out orders to his men to close ranks, as more and more of his own men cleared the ditch. A task made all the easier now that Spartacus had created a defensive wall to offer them cover. Seeing that the catapults had carved a breach as wide as fifty men standing abreast, that is where Spartacus chose to lead his men. He yelled is us orders, and slowly the shield wall moved forward, still receiving deadly missile fire. All speed was sacrificed for the sake of cohesion, they needed to stay as one unit, for it was only a matter of time before the defenders launched a counter attack. The slope made marching together difficult and so gaps naturally appeared in the line, it was here that the missiles found their targets, but quickly another man took the place of the fallen. Spartacus did not allow his men to stop they moved always forwards taking the best the enemy could throw at them. Suddenly the defenders were pulling back from the fortifications, aware that they could not stop the attackers with missiles they gathered just inside their compound to launch a crunching charge at the thin shield wall. Spartacus stopped his force right the centre of the breach. He had time to set his men, and made sure they could not be out flanked by forming the shield wall to eventually fill the entire breach.

'Stand firm, do not break ranks. Let them come to us,' Spartacus bellowed.

The Ordovice smashed into Spartacus line, for a moment it seemed his men must be overwhelmed, but after the initial shock where Spartacus' men were driven back a pace, the charge was halted. The gladius carried by Spartacus and his men was designed for just this type of warfare, it shot out from behind shield to gut the nearest Ordovice and then disappeared behind the shield once again. The Ordovice on the other hand carried weapons which were designed to be wielded upon the open battlefield, large swords and axes were of little use in such close quarter skirmishes. Before long the Ordovice were slipping on the blood of their fallen comrades and now they could see Dumnonii tribesmen filing from the ditch, keen on taking their heads. The speed in which a battle can change can be frightening, one minute the Ordovice were numerically superior and launching a ferocious charge the next they were fleeing for their lives trying to reach the secondary defences.

'Form up, do not chase the bastards,' yelled Spartacus.

He only just managed to hold the Dumnonii with him, clearly they wanted revenge for the years the Ordovice had subjected them to. He called for Plinius, who appeared at his shoulder,

'Plinius I want you to take this first wave of Dumnonii, along these fortifications. Clear the enemy out, if we clear the first line of defences then the Durotrige will be able join us all the quicker from the north side, understand?'

'Consider it done,' Plinius waved his hands to get the message across to Dumnonii warriors and off he sped, followed by eager men keen to kill Ordovice. Spartacus looked behind him and already the next wave of Dumnonii were starting to clear the ditch, so far the plan had worked well he thought.

'Get your breath back men, for in a moment we take the next defences.' He wanted to get the timing right, he needed to hit the next breach as the Dumnonii entered the first, that way, the obvious choice for them would be to hit the smaller breaches and created confusion for the defenders. It worked to perfection just has Spartacus held the main breach, the defenders carried out another defensive charge but that soon gave way, as hundreds of Dumnonii poured in through the smaller gaps in the defences. Many of the Ordovice were too slow in their retreat and were hacked to pieces by their vengeful enemy. The third line of defences had suffered no damage but the defenders themselves were lacking the numbers to defend its perimeter. As more and more Dumnonii joined the battle and then thousands of screaming Durotrige swarmed into the battle, both attacker and defender knew there could be only one outcome. The third line of defences fell easily and all the remnants of the defenders filtered into the last fortification of the fortress.

Spartacus and his allies took their time breathing heavily from their exertions, trying to force much needed air back into their lungs. Penduim appeared at his shoulder at the same time the Ordovice leader appeared upon in the battlements to curse his enemy and spit down his defiance.

'I take it he does not want to surrender?'

'No and to be honest, he knows we would not accept it anyway.'

'Then let's get this done.'

Penduim let out a terrifying war cry which was answered at once by all the attackers, as they burst into the charge and swarmed towards what was left of the Ordovice. The timbers were high in these defences and the attackers needed to use each other as human ladders to try and get into the stockade. Others merely began chopping at the defences with heavy axes, all the time the defenders tried their best to hold the tide back but to no avail. Spartacus landed upon the wooden defence work almost thrown bodily over the defences by Penduim and his men. He slipped as he landed and heard the cry of an attacking enemy coming from behind, he managed to throw himself to the side, a powerful axe just missing his skull. The mighty weapon came round again, and Spartacus had nowhere left to go and just as he thought his time in this world was over, an arrow shaft thudded into the warrior's throat and the axe fell harmlessly to the floor. Spartacus picked himself up and glanced over the battlements to see Tictus smiling up at him. Spartacus turned as a spear tip ripped through his shoulder, there in front of him was the Ordovice chieftain smiling his menace. The chieftain had already let go of the spear and was drawing his sword. Spartacus stumbled backwards and ripped the spear from his own body. The chieftain slashed at him, Spartacus parried the blow but the pain was almost unbearable and he could feel his body becoming weak rapidly. He did not have much time and decided to attack, the chieftain aimed another skull splitting cut at Spartacus who waited till the very last moment before ducking under the blow and came up immediately with his own blade. The chieftain' eyes went from anger to surprise and back to anger, as the two crashed down together both lost grip of their weapons and the chieftain his powerful hands clenched about Spartacus' throat. Lights exploded in Spartacus view and then slowly his world began to dim as he fought for breath. Suddenly his throat was released but the darkness continued and Spartacus lay slumped on the walkway oblivious to all that was happening around him.

Orin was searching the various buildings desperately searching for Flabinus and vengeance. He smashed through the doors of the meeting hall to be confronted by three dark clad men, obviously Flabinus' men.

'Where is he?' he part asked part screamed.

'Gone, your too late,' one of them replied.

Orin exploded with anger, every inch of his body yearned for revenge and at not being able to find the man responsible, he would take the next best thing his men. The suddenly fury of his attack took the men by surprise, one of which moved much too slowly, Orin took his head with one well placed back stroke. The others knew they were in a fight now and they tried to flank the man who fought like a demon. The meeting hall was dark, lit only by a small torch and in the fight it was knocked to the floor, and all light was extinguished the men fighting movement and shadows. For a time screams of anger and pain ruled but then fell a deathly silence. The door to the meeting hall slowly creaked opened, Plinius turned in case an enemy came at him, Orin stumbled to him and collapsed in his arms,

'I could not find Flabinus, I will not have my vengeance.'

'Quiet now, we must attend your wounds.'

'I took his men, they lie in the dust. Do you think my father will forgive my failure.'

'Your father loved you Orin, he will know of your bravery.' But as Plinius spoke his last words, the life left Orin. His eyes became shadows of what they had once been, Plinius laid him down gently upon the floor and closed his eyes. Plinius looked around to see all the dead and dying, Arthurax the Dumnonii who had challenged Spartacus lay upon the ground, his stomach had been opened by an Ordovice spear. Every where he looked familiar faces lay in the dust, skin pale and eyes vacant, he cursed the Gods for they demanded too much sacrifice, for just one man and still Flabinus evaded them. He called for his friends, for the battle was coming to an end. The remnant of the Ordovice army either pleaded for mercy or died with sword in hand. Some of the victors simply slumped to the floor exhaustion finally taking them, but many still craved revenge, and they delivered terrible retribution upon their vanquished foe. The allied tribes would take trophies, so the Ordovice not only lost the battle, their lives but also many lost their heads. Those collecting their trophies danced holding aloft the macabre proof of victory.

Chapter XXVII

Cassian and Aegis watched the proceedings, all seemed to be going well. Their thoughts now turned to that of their friends. Aegis finally lost his patience,

'I'm going to help with the wounded.'

'Of course yes,' replied Cassian 'fearing he had truly hurt his friend by making him stay behind.' Aegis pushed his horse on, glad to have the chance to be useful. Cassian watched him leave, then switched his sights back to the fortress and wondered whether Spartacus had found Flabinus and if the beast finally lay in the dirt where he belonged. Cassian was also finding all this waiting hard to stomach himself, and decided he would move closer. Wondering whether he should join Aegis in tending the wounded. He turned on his horse and called to the catapult crew,

'You have performed your actions with great skill today, I wonder would you be so kind as to set the fires, so the wounded may be cared for and hot meals for all.'

'Of course general.'

The soldier had meant it as a compliment, but it made Cassian wince,

'No please, my name is Cassian and I am no soldier. I would have no wish for this responsibility again.

'Sorry.'

'Nothing to be sorry for.'

Cassian turned and rode away. The soldier scratched his head and looked at the retreating figure of Cassian,

'Anyone would think he lost the bloody battle.'

Cassian slowed his mount wondering if Aegis actually wanted his company, he watched the big man as he rode towards a wounded soldier who had emerged from the ditch cradling his arm. For some reason Cassian could not take his eyes of the wounded man, who walked with such a strange gait. As Aegis approached him, the soldier fell and the old healer quickly jumped from his horse. Cassian noted how Aegis bent down keen to help the injured man, only to stand bolt upright almost immediately. Cassian was taken aback at what had happened and then as Aegis stumbled, the unmistakeable glint of a blade shone from the centre of his chest. For a moment Cassian was frozen, unable to move or utter a word, as he saw the soldier start to rise. Aegis slammed a fist into the man's face making him fall backwards. Aegis staggered towards his horse and slapped the beast to make it take flight, it was only then that Cassian recovered his senses and charged to his friend's aid. The soldier was back on his feet now, and drew another blade, Cassian willed Aegis to turn around and face his assailant. Aegis did not turn but merely stared to the heavens, the soldier took Aegis by the hair and drew his dagger across his throat. Cassian screamed, his entire body burned with anger. Even before his horse had come to a halt Cassian had leapt from it, and drawing his sword in one single movement. He stared across at Aegis' murderer and even before the man turned to face him he knew who stood before him. The figure reached up and removed his helmet,

'Well Cassian, it is fitting that we meet like this, don't you agree?'

'It was always going to be so.'

'Thing is I'm not sure you are up to the challenge, after all what can a man who has known only privilege and pampering hope to achieve against me.'

'Personally I just wish your throat was as big as your ego, then I could not miss.'

'There are no more friends to die for you here Cassian, not even another pretty little wife. I believe she had more fight in her than you do.'

'So stop talking and find out.'

The two men circled one another, Flabinus smiled he knew he was the better man. For his part Cassian knew that was the truth too, but all he needed was one chance, he would gladly offer his life to take the smile from that face. The first blows were exchanged and when the men parted, a cut had appeared upon Cassian' shoulder. Cassian tried to ignore the cut but by the Gods this man was quick, he tried to think like Spartacus, he moved faster trying to force Flabinus off balance. Another cut opened on Cassian's thigh and then another on his forearm.

'I'm running out of places to strike you Cassian.'

Cassian never replied, he could not out move the man so he must get in close. He danced one way and then the other, thinking all the time of what Spartacus had taught him, words filtered into his mind as if the great warrior had whispered them into his ear.

'There is no honour in a fight to the death, win and win at all costs.'

Another stinging cut across his cheek focussed his thoughts on what he must do, he moved even faster, until one last move brought him closer than he had ever been. He felt coldness of a blade at his side, and Flabinus smiled. Cassian forced himself on the blade breaking his flesh and piercing him just above his hip, as Flabinus stared in shock, Cassian threw his head into the man's face smashing his nose to pulp. Before Flabinus could wipe the tears and blood from his eyes Cassian brought his sword sweeping down and the sword arm of Flabinus fell to the ground. Flabinus screamed as Cassian kicked him in the chest, Flabinus scrambled and held out his hand for mercy, Cassian took it off, with a flick of his blade. More screams and now Flabinus lay curled on the floor begging for his life.

'The great Flabinus begging for his life, come now surely you have some master stroke of deceit that will get you out of this one. After all you are not yet dead.'

Spartacus opened his eyes, pain soared through his shoulder which had been dressed and his head throbbed, Penduim drifted into his sight.

'Thought that big bastard had done for me.'

'He would have if I hadn't twisted his head round the other way, it came as I shock to him I can tell you.'

'I'm sure it did, thank you.'

'How is the patient?' asked Cassian as he approached.

'I'd be better when you let a proper healer tend to me, where is Aegis.'

'He's gone my friend.' Cassia laid a hand upon Spartacus' good shoulder.

'But he wasn't even in the battle, how?'

'Can you walk?'

'Yes I think so,' replied Spartacus.

'Then come with me, I will show you the culprit.'

Neither of the men spoke as they made their way slowly through the large Ordovice compound, only stopping when they reached the large meeting house in which Orin had met his fate. More torches had been placed in the hall of the meeting house and as Spartacus' eyes accustomed themselves to the change in light, he became aware of men in the room. Plinius, Lathyrus, Melachus and Tictus all stood waiting for him, he was so glad to see they had come through the battle alive. Cassian pointed towards the centre of the room and there tied to the centre table lay a figure, that

Spartacus instantly guessed to be Flabinus. Cassian moved forward,

'I thought it necessary that we all witnessed what has become of the man who took so much from us. Cassian slapped the figure who groaned his displeasure, Flabinus I have brought friends to see you.'

'Just kill me,' the now broken Flabinus croaked.

'Oh I am afraid that the wounds you have suffered will kill you, though our healers did the best they could to dress the wounds and prevent further blood loss. I think only Aegis could have saved you, but you murdered him didn't you.'

'Do your worst when my brother hears of my fate he will hunt each and every one of you down.'

'That is indeed the mark of a loyal brother, it's a shame he is not here in your hour of need. One moment, he is let me fetch him.' Cassian ducked below the table bringing up a large leather bag. 'Like I said, it would be nice if he was here so…..' Cassian pulled the head of Dion from the bag the weeks had not been kind to it. He placed it upon the chest of Flabinus and then whispered,

'Did you think that you would simply walk away, you killed my wife and my friends, think on this, as you pass your last few hours in this world.' Cassian and his friends walked from the meeting hall, not one glanced back as Flabinus' screams rang out, it wouldn't be long before the broken fortress lay completely empty, it took Flabinus until just before dark to die, the loss of blood finally taking him, his last view of the world, the rotting head of his brother.

On the plain before the smashed fortress, a number of funeral pyres were constructed and as the sun went down Cassian and his men said goodbye to their fallen comrades. The last pyre to be lit was that of Aegis. Spartacus was reminded of when they had first met, and the skilled warrior and healer told Spartacus of his homeland.

'My home is no more, torn apart by wars that left only destruction. Gone are the chiefs, the soothsayers, the people, only dust remains and when I die my body will turn to such dust and the winds will blow me to rest, with my kin.'

Spartacus looked in to the flames smoke and ash drifted upon the breeze, he followed it briefly,

'Safe journey my friend, safe journey.'

The following day the army began its journey south, many had died the previous day and it was difficult to celebrate victory.

332

However despite the loss, there was something different amongst Cassian and his friends, the beast was gone, each day before the death of Flabinus was one of wondering. Never knowing whether or not that particular day was the one that you would die or worse those that you loved. The threat had been removed, and now all they craved was to be home, away from deceit, battle and death.

The days passed and when celebration at victory and the mourning of lost friends was complete, plans were made for Cassian and his men to leave. Goodbyes were heartily given and gifts passed from one party to another, and soon the vessels began their journey home. Penduim stood upon the hillside, next to him a figure dressed in black his face completely hidden.

'Will you bless their journey, for they have done much for our people.'

'Indeed they have, but I fear their journey will be long, and bring many trials.'

'Will they never get to rest?' Penduim shook his head.

'Perhaps one day, but the Gods have need of men as such as sail in those vessels.'

THE END

Historical Note

The journey of Spartacus and his friends within the novel was both arduous and long. It led them to experience new lands and the people of those lands. I have tried to remain constant with the historical writings in regards to both the varying people of the lands themselves.

Cyrene

An ancient city state which is located in present day Libya, settled originally by the Greeks in 630 B.C. It was over time ruled by the Ptolemaic dynasty with just a brief spell declaring its independence around 270 B.C, although was taken back under the Egyptian Ptolemaic control. It remained this way until it was bequeathed by Ptolemy Apion to Rome, the area becoming under Roman law in 96 B.C, however this was not formalised until 74 B.C. Under the former rulers the immigrant Judeans had enjoyed a peaceful and flourishing existence, however with the colony now under Roman rule the stability they once knew evaporated. The once influential people now found themselves second class citizens, being prevented from reaching high office. Within my book i have placed these troubles as the reason Dara and Orin seek the help of Flabinus, with terrible consequences. However in truth it took many years before the troubles would erupt into violence. Most notably in 73 AD and 117 AD where particularly in 117 AD many of the protagonists lost their lives. Indeed it is believed that Libya's population was so depleted by warfare that under the emperor Hadrian new settlements had to be created.

British Tribes

The novel is set in 69 B.C, and as such there were far too many tribes to give an account of them all. The Dumnonii has I have stated in the novel were a strange tribe without capital settlements and no ruling family to speak of. They occupied the part of Britain which is now known as Devon and Cornwall, some believe they were a collection of smaller tribes rather than one major tribe, maybe this is the reason for the lack of a central power. They traded with Brittany, however they did not use coin. When finally the Roman invasion did take place, it seems it hardly affected these tribes. It seems they simply allowed the Romans to govern their lands' evidence for this was the lack of Roman fortifications required in this area. In truth it would be unlikely that the average

Dumnonii felt that his life changed in any tangible way from pre-roman times.

The Durotriges from Wiltshire and Somerset were different to the Dumnonii in a few regards, they minted their own coin long before the Romans occupied and took much longer than most tribes to give up living in their hill forts. They traded with Gaul, however its importance to their economy did not have the weight of trade with other local tribes. They resisted the Roman invasion as best they could, it is believed they are one of the tribes that gave Vespasian so much trouble.

The Ordovices were different again, they were farmers who lived in basically fortified farms. They occupied the hills and mountains of what is now known as Wales. They were formidable fighters with very close relations with the Druids who were so hated by the Romans. They allied themselves with Caratacus who became their warlord, and put up a spirited defiance of Rome. However at Caratacus was defeated and the Ordovices became less of a threat, probably due to the amount of losses suffered by the tribe. Tacitus states that in the 70's AD (exact year unknown) the Ordovices had once again become rebellious so much so that the Roman governor Agricola ordered them exterminated. Could he have carried out such a feat when the enemy lived in such remote lands, it seems unlikely however there would be no further mention of the Ordovices in history. I have tried to be accurate within the novel and true to history but please forgive me if there are errors, but then history is an interpretation of truth even by the finest minds.

Coming Soon

Wrath of the Furies

Deep inside the mind of man, sits the abyss in which all reason and sanity can cascade to nothingness. Often men visit this ominous place, timidly peering over the edge as a child sneaks a look over the rail of a bridge. However, a catalyst so great and profound can force the man further, tipping him from the reality of this world, towards the darkness. He gazes into the void, searching for what is lost, but only sees the spectral beasts, laughing and chastising his futility. They become pivotal to his being, the blame and anger he feels swells, almost too bursting point; he must release the pressure. Each moment experienced in the darkness fuels his obsession, driving his anger forward to an act with must

take place. If only for a moment he would glance to a gentle stream

and observe his reflection, then the dark monster staring back may

sway his mind from the deeds he is committed to. There is of

course no time for reflections of any type, the journey is set. A

beast shall hunt beasts, and the innocent should try to stay clear.

116 A.D is coming to an end; the snows are not far away and

on the outskirts of the huge Roman Empire its fighting men, pray

for a quiet winter. The 9th legion was no different, tired of chasing

ghostly barbarians day after day, the effort bringing them to the

point of exhaustion. They yearned for the warmth of a bed and a

good meal, the more seasoned troops of which there were many in

the ranks of the 9th kept the more inexperienced troops moving

forward. An example of both stood at the track side as the legion

filed by, centurion Lentulus passed the wine to his superior and

smiled. The old centurion liked the man; he could not help it. He

was in no doubt that the young man was no soldier and had no real

wish to be here, but then which of them did. His superior

approached each task with enthusiasm if not skill. Unusually, he was also more than comfortable when it came to asking for advice, a rarity for those of a more privileged background.

'We will not reach the main garrison before nightfall,' spat the old centurion.

'Another night wallowing like swine in the mud then Lentulus,' replied Aelius, as he fingered a pendant which hung about his neck. While he spoke he watched a small bird hopping in and out of the deep divots left by the marching army. The creature clearly searched for a tasty morsel, it seemed to look back at the officer as if thanking him for the meal provided. It eagerly pecked at a partly unearthed worm. Then the bird spread its wings and took off soaring into the skies above, Aelius watched it disappear into the clouds, and for a moment wished that he too could simply take flight. Leave forever the life of soldiering with all its filth and death, for the cleansing beauty of the clouds above.

'After sixteen years serving in the legions mud passes for an old friend,' Lentulus interrupted the thoughts of his commanding officer.

'Not sure I will ever get used to it, and I have to admit all this marching is getting a little tedious.'

'I share your boredom. So tomorrow why don't we change things a little, we could join the scouts. It's a little more interesting in the way of work and will give you some valuable experience.'

'Is it normal for my rank to leave the main column?'

'It is normal for those who want to be better at what they do.'

'Very well, thank you Lentulus your support has been invaluable these last few months.'

'No need for thanks, as you say, years of marching become a little tedious. I was grateful for the distraction.'

As the ninth legion slowed and then finally came to a halt for the night, it was exhausted soldiers who wearily secured the temporary camp for the night. Their plight made all the more miserable for the light rain which accompanied the bitterly cold winter breeze which stung any exposed flesh. The men clambered into their small tents; eight men slept in each and in weather such as this, they were glad of it. The warmth from each soldier warmed the next, Aelius and Lentulus however, were afforded more spacious accommodation and contented themselves by warming from within. Wine was consumed until exhaustion took them, and they slipped into much-needed and earned slumber.

The following morning the rains had stopped to be replaced by a dense spectral mist that wrapped itself ominous around the sleeping legion. Lentulus shook Aelius from his sleep, informing his superior that he had collected a pair of mounts, and that they should prepare to leave. It took time for Aelius to shake the morning weariness from his muscles, but as time went on, and as they left the legion further behind, he began to become aware of the mood of Lentulus. The centurion was unusually high spirited; he laughed and joked, seemingly unconcerned that an enemy may well be lurking near. Both men and their horses climbed a steep incline covered in small trees, and on reaching its summit turned to observe the finest fighting men Rome had to offer.

'It will not be long before they begin to march again.'

'That is true, but the scouts are set and with have time,' Lentulus paused, 'and knowing you to like a hearty breakfast, I have managed to obtain some fine cuts of beef.'

'But shouldn't we keep watch?' replied Aelius.

'Our men cover these hills; they see all that we see. Besides you will learn more by observing from this position. Shall I raise a fire or do you wish this food to go to waste?'

Aelius did not reply but with one last look at the army below, he climbed from his mount. Lentulus barked out his laughter, and joined his friend to prepare the fire. They talked for some time as they enjoyed the succulent meat, while observing the legion breaking camp and moving along the track which led into woodland. Trees now began to obstruct their view, and only glimpses of the great line of fighting men could be observed among the canopy of greenery. Onwards the legion marched becoming harder for Aelius to discern their exact location, until at last something else caught his attention. To the rear of the legion, he had seen movement, stragglers his first thought but for some unknown reason he could not remove his eyes from the area. Larger and larger his eyes became as stark realisation dawned upon him, there in numbers that could only be estimated in the thousands, barbarians swarmed towards the rear of the legion. Aelius grasped Lentulus by the shoulder forcing the centurion to look at the terrible sight.

'We must warn the legion,' Aelius blurted.

'No wait, we must be sure of our facts. Look there beyond the legions left flank.'

Aelius' jaw dropped in utter dismay as yet more barbarians streamed towards the exposed flanks of the legions. As they continue to witness yet more bands of warriors could be seen closing upon the men of Rome, the trap had been sprung, and only the Gods could save the men of the ninth now. For some time, the two stood watching as the warrior bands closed in and then the unmistakable sound of battle, the stunned Aelius finally managed to mutter,

'Lentulus what do we do?'

'There would be no point going down there, the fight was lost before it commenced. So I suppose the main garrison should be informed.'

'How could this happen? The trap was laid in advance they were too well prepared.'

'Coin, loosens tongues Aelius. A soldier, trader or senator there are always men willing to betray for a profit.'

'We should ride; those that need to know about this carnage had better receive the news quickly.'

'I wish that was possible Aelius.'

Aelius was confused by the response, his confusion turning shock as the flash of a blade passed before his sight. The pain was almost unreal at first, the man's mind not willing to interpret it as such. He looked down as the scarlet ooze began to stream along his arm, and as it fell so did he, the strength leaving his legs. He raised his head to look at the centurion before him,

'Why?'

'Sixteen years marching in mud Aelius, believe me, it does not become a companion. I was offered a tidy sum to help a man supply those victorious warriors down there with weapons. I must say they have learnt to use them quickly; the second payment I took was to ensure the death of a certain man. Now battles can be unpredictable, and so it was important that I could prove I was responsible for the young man's death.'

'I thought you were……'

'Your friend? In truth you are a fine man Aelius, and I regret this act. However, a deal has been struck and failure to carry out the deed would result in my own death.'

The blade sort out flesh again and the young soldier Aelius gasped his final breath. Lentulus reached down and tore the pendant that Aelius never removed from his person, and so the centurion had his proof. A small brown bird landed just a few steps from the crumpled body of Aelius and the treacherous centurion. It stared meaningfully at the fallen young man and gave a sorrowful shriek and then was gone returning to the clouds above. Lentulus watched the creature go, it unsettled the veteran soldier of so many campaigns, he so desperately wanted to leave this place. With one last look at the man he had robbed of life, a lingering stare which was filled with regret and he too like the bird left the place. The land was no longer a place for the living, cursed by the Gods, testament to man's treachery and barbarity. It would be many days before the main garrison would hear the news of the fallen legion, and many more before the disaster would be learnt of in Rome. The soldiers of the ninth legion would not be afforded burial or funeral pyres, and so they became nourishment for the beast and carrion. Only one Roman survived the slaughter, and he slipped away into the hills, to meet his master the real architect of the legion's downfall.

Lightning Source UK Ltd.
Milton Keynes UK
UKOW05f2026161013

219201UK00001B/7/P